The Everyman Wodehouse

P. G. WODEHOUSE

# Over Seventy

*An Autobiography with Digressions*

EVERYMAN

Published by Everyman's Library
Northburgh House
10 Northburgh Street
London EC1V 0AT

Originally published in the USA in a different version entitled *America, I Like You*
by Simon & Schuster, New York, 1956
Rewritten edition published in Great Britain as *Over Seventy: An Autobiography
with Digressions* by Herbert Jenkins Ltd, London, 1957
Published by Everyman's Library, 2014
This edition reprints the 1957 text.

Typography by Peter B. Willberg

ISBN 978-1-84159-194-0

A CIP catalogue record for this book is available from the British Library

Distributed by Random House (UK) Ltd.,
20 Vauxhall Bridge Road, London SW1V 2SA

Typeset by AccComputing, Wincanton, Somerset
Printed and bound in Germany
by CPI books GmbH, Leck

# Over Seventy

# CONTENTS

There is a rare treat in store for the reader[1] of this book. Except in the Foreword,[2] which will soon be over, it is entirely free from footnotes.

I am not, I think, an irascible man,[3] but after reading a number of recent biographies and histories I have begun to feel pretty sore about these footnotes and not in the mood to be put upon much longer.[4] It is high time,[5] in my opinion, that this nuisance was abated and biographers and essayists restrained from strewing these unsightly blemishes[6] through their pages as if they were ploughing the fields and scattering the good seed o'er the land.[7]

I see no need for the bally things.[8] I have just finished reading Carl Sandburg's *Abraham Lincoln, The War Years*, and Carl manages to fill four fat volumes without once resorting to this exasperating practice.[9] If he can do it, why can't everyone?[10]

1 Or readers. Let's be optimistic.
2 Sometimes called Preface. See *Romeo and Juliet*, Act Two, Scene One – 'A rose by any other name would smell as sweet'.
3 Sunny Jim, many people call me.
4 See *King Lear*, Act One, Scene Two – 'Some villain hath done me wrong'.
5 Greenwich Mean or, in America, Eastern Standard.
6 Footnotes.
7 Hymns A. and M.
8 Footnotes.
9 Bunging in a footnote every second paragraph.
10 Answer me that.

Frank Sullivan, the American writer,[11] has already raised his voice[12] on this subject,[13] being particularly severe on the historian Gibbon for his habit of getting you all worked up, thinking now that you are going to hear full details of the vices of the later Roman emperors, and then switching you off to a Latin footnote which defies translation for the ordinary man who forgot all the Latin he ever knew back in 1920.[14]

I know just how Frank feels. It is the same with me. When I read a book I am like someone strolling across a level lawn, thinking how jolly it all is, and when I am suddenly confronted with a [1] or a [2] it is as though I had stepped on the teeth of a rake and had the handle spring up and hit me on the bridge of the nose. I stop dead and my eyes flicker and swivel. I tell myself that this time I will not be fooled into looking at the beastly thing,[15] but I always am, and it nearly always maddens me by beginning with the word 'see'. 'See the *Reader's Digest*, April 1950,' says one writer on page 7 of his latest work, and again on page 181, 'See the *Reader's Digest*, October 1940.'

How do you mean, 'See' it, my good fellow?[16] Are you under the impression that I am a regular subscriber to the *Reader's Digest* and save up all the back numbers? Let me tell you that if in the waiting-room of my dentist or some such place my eye falls on a copy of this widely circulated little periodical, I wince

11 One of the Saratoga, N.Y., Sullivans.
12 A light baritone, a little uncertain in the upper register.
13 Footnotes.
14 Or, in my case, earlier. The sort of thing Sullivan dislikes is when Gibbon says you simply wouldn't believe the things the Empress Theodora used to get up to, and tells you in the footnote that she was *in tres partes divisa* and much given to the *argumentum ad hominem et usque ad hoc.*
15 The footnote.
16 The man's an ass.

away from it like a salted snail, knowing that in it lurks some ghastly Most Unforgettable Character I Ever Met.

Slightly, but not much, better than the footnotes which jerk your eye to the bottom of the page are those which are lumped together somewhere in the back of the book. These allow of continuous reading, or at any rate are supposed to, but it is only a man of iron will who, coming on a [6] or a [7], can keep from dropping everything and bounding off after it like a basset hound after a basset.[17]

This involves turning back to ascertain which chapter you are on, turning forward and finding yourself in the Index, turning back and fetching up on Sources, turning forward and getting entangled in Bibliography and only at long last hooking the Notes; and how seldom the result is worth the trouble. I was reading the other day that bit in Carrington's *Life of Rudyard Kipling* where Kipling and his uncle Fred Macdonald go to America and Kipling tries to sneak in incog. and Fred Macdonald gives him away to the reporters. When I saw a [7] appended to this I was all keyed up. Now, I felt, we're going to get something good. The footnote, I told myself, will reveal in detail what Kipling said to Fred Macdonald about his fatheadedness and I shall pick up some powerful epithets invaluable for use in conversations with taxi-drivers and traffic policemen.

Here is [7] *in toto*:

#### F. W. MACDONALD

If that is not asking for bread and being given a stone, it would be interesting to know what it is. The only thing you can say for a footnote like that is that it is not dragged in, as are most

---

17 What *is* a basset? I've often wondered.

footnotes, just to show off the writer's erudition, as when the author of – say – *The Life of Sir Leonard Hutton* says:

It was in the pavilion at Leeds – not, as has sometimes been stated, at Manchester – that Sir Leonard first uttered those memorable words, 'I've been having a spot of trouble with my lumbago.'

and then with a [6] directs you to the foot of the page, where you find:

Unlike Giraldus Cambrensis, who in *Happy Days at Bognor Regis* mentions suffering from measles and chickenpox as a child but says that he never had lumbago. See also Caecilius Status, Dio Chrysostom and Abu Mohammed Kasim Ben Ali Hariri.

Which is intolerable.[18]

No footnotes, then, in this book of mine, and I think on the whole no Dedication.

Nobody seems to be doing these now, and it just shows how things have changed since the days when I was starting out to give a shot in the arm to English Literature. At the turn of the century the Dedication was the thing on which we authors all spread ourselves. It was the *bonne bouche* and the *sine qua non*.

We went in for variety in those days. When you opened a novel, you never knew what you were going to get. It might be the curt, take-it-or-leave-it dedication:

To
J. Smith

and the somewhat warmer:

To
My friend Percy Brown

18 It is what Shakespeare would have called a fardel. See *Hamlet*, Act Three, Scene One – 'Who would fardels bear?'

one of those cryptic things with a bit of poetry in italics:

To
F.B.O.

*Stark winds*
*And sunset over the moors*
*Why?*
*Whither?*
*Whence?*
*And the roll of distant drums*

or possibly the nasty dedication, intended to sting:

To
J. Alastair Frisby
Who Told Me I Would Never Have A Book Published
And
Advised me
To
Get a job selling jellied eels
SUCKSTOYOU, FRISBY

It was all great fun and kept our pores open and our blood circulating, but it is not difficult to see why the custom died out. Inevitably a time came when there crept into authors' minds the question, 'What is there in this for me?' I know it was so in my own case. 'What is Wodehouse getting out of this?' I asked myself, and the answer, as far as I could see, was, 'Not a thing.'

When the eighteenth-century author inserted on page 1 something like

To
The Most Noble and Puissant Lord Knubble of Knopp
This book is dedicated
By His very Humble Servant, the Author

My Lord,

It is with inexpressible admiration for your lordship's transcendent gifts that the poor slob who now addresses your lordship presents to your lordship this trifling work, so unworthy of your lordship's distinguished consideration,

he expected to do himself a bit of good. Lord Knubble was his patron and could be relied on, unless having one of his attacks of gout, to come through with at least a couple of guineas. But where does a modern author like myself get off? I pluck – let us say – P. B. Biffen from the ranks of the unsung millions and make him immortal, and what does Biffen do in return? He does nothing. He just stands there. I probably won't get so much as a lunch out of it.

So no Dedication and, as I say, none of those obscene little fly-specks scattered about all over the page.[19]

I must conclude by expressing my gratitude to Mr P. G. Wodehouse for giving me permission to include in these pages an extract from his book, *Louder and Funnier*. Pretty decent of him, I call it.[20]

Here ends the Foreword. Now we're off.

19 Footnotes.
20 The whitest man I know.

I

Interesting letter the other day from J. P. Winkler.

You don't know J. P. Winkler? Nor, as a matter of fact, though he addresses me as friend, do I, but he seems to be a man of enterprise and a go-getter.

He says, writing from out Chicago way:

Friend Wodehouse,

For some time I have been presenting in newspapers and on radio a feature entitled *Over Seventy*, being expressions on living by those who have passed their seventieth year, and I should like to include you in this series.

Here are some of the questions I would like you to answer. What changes do you notice particularly in your daily life now? What changes in the American scene? Have you a regimen for health? Are you influenced by criticism of your books? Have you ever written poetry? Have you ever lectured? What do you think of television and the motion pictures?

I see you are living in the country now. Do you prefer it to the city? Give us the overall picture of your home life and describe your methods of work. And any information concerning your experiences in the theatre and any observations on life in general, as seen from the angle of over seventy, will be welcome.

You have been doing much these last fifty years, perhaps you can tell us something about it.

Naturally I was flattered, for we all know that it isn't everybody who gets included in a series. Nevertheless, that 'fifty years' piqued me a little. Long before fifty years ago I was leaving footprints on the sands of time, and good large footprints at that. In my early twenties it would not be too much to say that I was the talk of London. If you had not seen me riding my bicycle down the Strand to the offices of the *Globe* newspaper, where I was at that time employed, frequently using no hands and sometimes bending over to pick up a handkerchief with my teeth, it was pretty generally agreed that you had not seen anything. And the public's memory must be very short if the 22 not out I made for the printers of the *Globe* against the printers of the *Evening News* one Sunday in 1904 has been forgotten.

However, I get the idea, Winkler. You want to start the old gaffer mumbling away in the chimney corner over his clay pipe in the hope that something will emerge which you can present in newspapers and on radio. You would have me survey mankind from China to Peru, touching now on this subject, now on that, like a butterfly flitting from flower to flower, and every now and then coming up with some red-hot personal stuff by way of supplying the human interest.

Right ho. Let's get cracking and see what we can do about it.

## II

I am relieved, old man, that you do not insist on the thing being exclusively autobiographical, for as an autobiographer I am rather badly handicapped.

On several occasions it has been suggested to me that I might take a pop at writing my reminiscences. 'Yours has been a long life,' people say. 'You look about a hundred and four. You should make a book of it and cash in.'

It's a thought, of course, but I don't see how I could do it. The three essentials for an autobiography are that its compiler shall have had an eccentric father, a miserable misunderstood childhood and a hell of a time at his public school, and I enjoyed none of these advantages. My father was as normal as rice pudding, my childhood went like a breeze from start to finish, with everybody I met understanding me perfectly, while as for my schooldays at Dulwich they were just six years of unbroken bliss. It would be laughable for me to attempt a formal autobiography. I have not got the material. Anything on the lines of

Wodehouse, The Story of a Wonder Man

starting with

Chapter One: The Infant
Chapter Two: Childhood Days
Chapter Three: Sturm und Drang of Adolescence

is, I feel, out of the question.

Another thing about an autobiography is that, to attract the cash customers, it must be full of good stories about the famous, and I never can think of any. If it were just a matter of dropping names, I could do that with the best of them, but mere name-dropping is not enough. You have to have the sparkling anecdote as well, and any I could provide would be like the one Young Griffo, the boxer, told me in 1904 about his meeting with Joe Gans, the then lightweight champion. Having just been matched to fight Gans, he was naturally anxious to get a look at him before the formal proceedings began, and here is how he told the dramatic tale of their encounter.

'I was going over to Philadelphia to see a fight,' he said, 'and my manager asks me would I like to meet Joe Gans. He asks me if I like to meet Joe Gans, see, and I said I would. So we arrive in Philadelphia and we start out for one of the big sporting places where the gang all held out, and my manager asks me again do I want to see Joe Gans, and I say I do. So we go to this big sporting place where the gang all held out, and there's a big crowd standing around one of the tables, and somebody asks me would I like to meet Joe Gans, he's over at that table. Would I like to meet Joe Gans, he says, he's over at that table, he says, and I say I would. So he takes me to the table and says 'Here's Young Griffo, Joe,' he says. 'He wants to meet you,' he says. And sure enough it was Joe all right. He gets up from the table and comes right at me.'

I was leaning forward by this time and clutching the arms of my chair. How cleverly, I thought, just as if he had been a professional author, this rather untutored man had led up to the big moment.

'Yes?' I gasped. 'And then?'

'Huh?'

'What happened then?'

'He shakes hands with me. "Hullo, Griff," he says. And I say "Hullo, Joe".'

That was all. You might have thought more was coming, but no. He had met Gans, Gans had met him. It was the end of the story. My autobiography would be full of stuff like that.

'I had long wished to make the acquaintance of Mr (now Lord) Attlee, but it was not for some years that I was enabled to gratify this ambition. A friend took me to the House of Commons, and we were enjoying tea on the terrace when Mr Attlee came by.

'Oh, Clem,' said my friend, 'I want you to meet Mr Wodehouse.'

'How do you do?' said Mr Attlee.
'How do you do?' I replied.

You can't charge people sixteen bob or whatever it is for that sort of thing.

Still, I quite see, J.P., that I must give you something personal on which your radio public can chew, or we shall have them kicking holes in their sets. I could mention, for instance, that when I was four years old I used to play with an orange, but I doubt if that would interest them, and that at the age of six I read the whole of Pope's *Iliad*, which of course they wouldn't believe. Better, I think, to skip childhood and adolescence and go straight to the Autumn of 1900, when, a comely youth of some eighteen summers, I accepted employment in the Lombard Street office of the Hong Kong and Shanghai Bank. Reluctantly, I may mention. As the song says, I didn't want to do it, I didn't want to do it, but my hand was forced.

The trouble in the Wodehouse home at the beginning of the century was that money was a good deal tighter than could have been wished. The wolf was not actually whining at the door and there was always a little something in the kitty for the butcher and the grocer, but the finances would not run to anything in the nature of a splash. My father, after many years in Hong Kong, had retired on a pension, and the authorities paid it to him in rupees. A thoroughly dirty trick, in my opinion, for the rupee is the last thing in the world – or was then – with which anyone who valued his peace of mind would wish to be associated. It never stayed put for a second. It was always jumping up and down and throwing fits, and expenditure had to be regulated in the light of what mood it happened to be in at the moment. 'Watch that rupee!' was the cry in the Wodehouse family.

The result was that during my schooldays my future was

always uncertain. The Boy, What Will He Become? was a question that received a different answer almost daily. My brother Armine had got a scholarship and gone to Oxford, and the idea was that, if I got a scholarship too, I would join him there. All through my last term at Dulwich I sprang from my bed at five sharp each morning, ate a couple of *petit beurre* biscuits and worked like a beaver at my Homer and Thucydides, but just as scholarship time was approaching, with me full to the brim with classic lore and just spoiling for a good whack at the examiners, the rupee started creating again, and it seemed to my father that two sons at the University would be a son more than the privy purse could handle. So Learning drew the loser's end, and Commerce got me.

You are probably thinking, Winkler, that this was a nice slice of luck for Commerce, but you are wrong. Possibly because I was a dedicated literary artist with a soul above huckstering or possibly – this was the view more widely held in the office – because I was just a plain dumb brick, I proved to be the most inefficient clerk whose trouser seat ever polished the surface of a high stool. I was all right as long as they kept me in the postal department, where I had nothing to do but stamp and post letters, a task for which my abilities well fitted me, but when they took me out of there and put me in Fixed Deposits the whisper went round Lombard Street, 'Wodehouse is at a loss. He cannot cope.'

If there was a moment in the course of my banking career when I had the foggiest notion of what it was all about, I am unable to recall it. From Fixed Deposits I drifted to Inward Bills – no use asking me what inward bills are. I never found out – and then to Outward Bills and to Cash, always with a weak, apologetic smile on my face and hoping that suavity of manner would see me through when, as I knew must happen 'ere long,

I fell short in the performance of my mystic duties. My total inability to grasp what was going on made me something of a legend in the place. Years afterwards, when the ineptness of a new clerk was under discussion in the manager's inner sanctum and the disposition of those present at the conference was to condemn him as the worst bungler who had ever entered the Hong Kong and Shanghai Bank's portals, some white-haired veteran in charge of one of the departments would shake his head and murmur, 'No, no, you're wrong. Young Robinson is, I agree, an almost total loss and ought to have been chloroformed at birth, but you should have seen P. G. Wodehouse. Ah, they don't make them like that nowadays. They've lost the pattern.'

Only two things connected with the banking industry did I really get into my head. One was that from now on all I would be able to afford in the way of lunch would be a roll and butter and a cup of coffee, a discovery which, after the lavish midday meals of school, shook me to my foundations. The other was that, if I got to the office late three mornings in a month, I would lose my Christmas bonus. One of the great sights in the City in the years 1901–2 was me rounding into the straight with my coat-tails flying and my feet going pitter pitter pat and just making it across the threshold while thousands cheered. It kept me in superb condition, and gave me a rare appetite for the daily roll and butter.

Owing to this slowness of uptake where commerce was concerned, I was never very happy in the bank, though probably happier than the heads of the various departments through which I made my stumbling way. What I would have liked to do on leaving school was to dig in at home and concentrate on my writing. My parents were living in Shropshire – lovely scenery and Blandings Castle just round the corner – and nothing would have suited me better than to withdraw to that earthly Paradise and devote myself to turning out short stories, which I used to do at that time at the rate of one a day. (In the summer of 1901 I contracted mumps and went home to have them in the bosom of my family. I was there three weeks, swelling all the time, and wrote nineteen short stories, all of which, I regret to say, editors were compelled to decline owing to lack of space. The editors regretted it, too. They said so.)

Putting this project up to my parents, I found them cold towards it. The cross all young writers have to bear is that, while they know that they are going to be spectacularly successful some day, they find it impossible to convince their nearest and dearest that they will ever amount to a row of beans. Write in your spare time, if you really must write, parents say, and they pull that old one about literature being a good something but a bad crutch. I do not blame mine for feeling that a son in a bank making his £80 a year, just like finding it in the street, was a sounder commercial proposition than one living at home and spending a fortune on stamps. (The editor is always glad to consider contributions, but a stamped and addressed envelope should be enclosed in case of rejection.)

So for two years I continued to pass my days in Lombard Street and write at night in my bed-sitting-room, and a testing experience it was, for all I got out of it was a collection of rejection slips with which I could have papered the walls of a good-sized banqueting hall. The best you could say of these was that some of them were rather pretty. I am thinking chiefly of the ones *Tit-Bits* used to send out, with a picture of the Newnes' offices in an attractive shade of green. I like those. But what I always feel about rejection slips is that their glamour soon wears off. When you've seen one, I often say, you've seen them all.

The handicap under which most beginning writers struggle is that they don't know how to write. I was no exception to this rule. Worse bilge than mine may have been submitted to the editors of London in 1901 and 1902, but I should think it very unlikely. I was sorry for myself at the time, when the stamped and addressed envelopes came homing back to me, but my sympathy now is for the men who had to read my contributions. I can imagine nothing more depressing than being an editor and coming to the office on a rainy morning in February with a nail in one shoe and damp trouser legs and finding oneself confronted with an early Wodehouse – written, to make it more difficult, in longhand.

H. G. Wells in his autobiography says that he was much influenced at the outset of his career by a book by J. M. Barrie called *When A Man's Single*. So was I. It was all about authors and journalists and it urged young writers to write not what they liked but what editors liked, and it seemed to me that I had discovered the prime grand secret. The result was that I avoided the humorous story, which was where my inclinations lay, and went in exclusively for the mushy sentiment which, judging from the magazines, was the thing most likely to bring a sparkle into an editor's eyes. It never worked. My only successes were with two-line He and She jokes for the baser weeklies.

*At The Servants' Ball*

COUNTESS (waltzing with her butler): I'm afraid I must stop, Wilber-force. I'm so danced out.
BUTLER: Oh, no, m'lady, just pleasantly so.

I got 1s. for that, and I still think it ought to have been 1s. 6d.

The curious thing about those early days is that, in spite of the blizzard of rejection slips, I had the most complete confidence in myself. I knew I was good. It was only later that doubts on this point began to creep in and to burgeon as time went by. Today I am a mass of diffidence and I-wonder-if-this-is-going-to-be-all-right-ness, and I envy those tough authors, square-jawed and spitting out of the side of their mouths, who are perfectly sure, every time they start a new book, that it will be a masterpiece. My own attitude resembles that of Bill, my foxhound, when he brings a decaying bone into the dining-room at lunch-time.

'Will this one go?' he seems to be saying, as he eyes us anxiously. 'Will my public consider this bone the sort of bone they have been led to expect from me, or will there be a sense of disappointment and the verdict that William is slipping?'

As a matter of fact, each of Bill's bones is just as dynamic and compelling as the last one, and he has nothing to fear at the bar of critical opinion, but with each new book of mine I have, as I say, always that feeling that this time I have picked a lemon in the garden of literature. A good thing, really, I suppose. Keeps one up on one's toes and makes one write every sentence ten times. Or in many cases twenty times. My books may not be the sort of books the cognoscenti feel justified in blowing the 12s. 6d. on, but I do work at them. When in due course Charon ferries me across the Styx and everyone is telling everyone else what a rotten writer I was, I hope at least one voice will be heard piping up, 'But he did take trouble.'

## III

I was getting, then, in the years 1901–2, so little audience response from the men in the editorial chairs that it began to seem that I might have done better to have taken up in my spare time some such hobby as fretwork or collecting bus tickets. But if only a writer keeps on writing, something generally breaks eventually. I had been working assiduously for eighteen months, glued to my chair and taking no part in London's night life except for a weekly dinner – half a crown and 6*d.* for the waiter – at the Trocadero grill-room, when somebody started a magazine for boys called the *Public School Magazine*, and on top of that came another called *The Captain*, and I had a market for the only sort of work I could do reasonably well – articles and short stories about school life. Wodehouse Preferred, until then down in the cellar with no takers, began to rise a bit. *The Public School Magazine* paid 10*s. 6d.* for an article and *The Captain* as much as £3 for a short story, and as I was now getting an occasional guinea from *Tit-Bits* and *Answers* I was becoming something of a capitalist. So much so that I began to have thoughts of resigning from the bank and using literature not as a whatever-it-is but as a crutch, especially as it would not be long now before I would be getting my orders.

The London office of the Hong Kong and Shanghai Bank was a sort of kindergarten where the personnel learned their jobs. At the end of two years, presumably by that time having learned them, they were sent out East to Bombay, Bangkok, Batavia and suchlike places. This was called getting one's orders, and the thought of getting mine scared the pants off me. As far as I could make out, when you were sent East you immediately became a branch manager or something of that sort, and the picture of myself managing a branch was one I preferred not to examine too closely. I couldn't have managed a whelk-stall.

And what of my Art? I knew in a vague sort of way that there were writers who had done well writing of life in foreign parts, but I could not see myself making a success of it. My line was good sound English stuff, the kind of thing the magazines liked

– stories of rich girls who wanted to be loved for themselves alone, and escaped convicts breaking into lonely country houses on Christmas Eve, when the white snow lay all around, and articles for *Tit-Bits* and school stories for *The Captain*. Could I carry on with these, enclosing a stamped addressed envelope in case of rejection, if I were out in Singapore or Sourabaya?

I thought not and, as I say, toyed with the idea of resigning. And then one day the thing was taken out of my hands and the decision made for me.

Let me tell you the story of the new ledger.

# IV

One of the things that sour authors, as every author knows, is being asked by people to write something clever in the front pages of their books. It was, I believe, George Eliot who in a moment of despondency made this rather bitter entry in her diary:

Dear Diary, am I a wreck tonight! I feel I never want to see another great admirer of my work again. It's not writing novels that's hard. I can write novels till the cows come home. What slays you is this gosh-darned autographing. 'Oh, *please!* Not just your *name*. Won't you write something *clever*.' I wish the whole bunch of them were in gaol, and I'd laugh myself sick if the gaol burned down.

And Richard Powell, the whodunit author, was complaining of this in a recent issue of *The American Writer*. 'I begin sweating,' he said, 'as soon as someone approaches me with a copy of one of my books.'

I feel the same. When I write a book, the golden words come pouring out like syrup, but let a smiling woman steal up to me with my latest and ask me to dash off something clever on the front page, and it is as though some hidden hand had removed my brain and substituted for it an order of cauliflower. There may be authors capable of writing something clever on the spur of the moment, but I am not of their number. I like at least a month's notice, and even then I don't guarantee anything.

Sometimes the quickness of the hand will get me by, but not often. When I am not typing I use one of those pen-pencil things which call for no blotting paper. The ink, or whatever the substance is that comes out at the top, dries as you write, so I take the book and scribble, 'Best wishes, P. G. Wodehouse' and with equal haste slam the lid, hoping that the party of the second part will have the decency not to peer inside till I am well out of the way. It seldom happens. Nine times out of ten she snaps the thing open like a waiter opening an oyster, and then the disappointed look, the awkward pause and the pained, 'But I wanted something *clever*.'[1]

The only time I ever wrote anything really clever on the front page of a book was when I was in the cash department of the Hong Kong and Shanghai Bank and a new ledger came in and was placed in my charge. It had a white, gleaming front page and suddenly, as I sat gazing at it, there floated into my mind like drifting thistledown the idea of writing on it a richly comic description of the celebrations and rejoicings marking the Formal Opening of the New Ledger, and I immediately proceeded to do so.

It was the most terrific 'piece', as they call it now. Though fifty-five years have passed since that day, it is still green in my memory.

---

1 I'm frightfully sorry, but I must have just one footnote here. I have recently taken to inscribing these books with the legend:
  'You like my little stories do ya?
  Oh, glory glory hallelujah.'
It sometimes goes well, sometimes not.

It had everything. There was a bit about my being presented to his Gracious Majesty the King (who, of course, attended the function) which would have had you gasping with mirth. ('From his tie he took a diamond tie-pin, and smiled at me, and then he put it back.') And that was just one passing incident in it. The whole thing was a knock-out. I can't give the details. You will have to take my word for it that it was one of the most screamingly funny things ever written. I sat back on my stool and felt like Dickens when he had finished *Pickwick*. I was all in a glow.

Then came the reaction. The head cashier was rather an austere man who on several occasions had expressed dissatisfaction with the young Wodehouse, and something seemed to whisper to me that, good as the thing was, it would not go any too well with him. Briefly, I got cold feet and started to turn stones and explore avenues in the hope of finding some way of making everything pleasant for all concerned. In the end I decided that the best thing to do was to cut the page out with a sharp knife.

A few mornings later the stillness of the bank was shattered by a sudden yell of triumph, not unlike the cry of the Brazilian wild cat leaping on its prey. It was the head cashier discovering the absence of the page, and the reason he yelled triumphantly was that he was feuding with the stationers and for weeks had been trying to get the goods on them in some way. He was at the telephone in two strides, asking them if they called themselves stationers. I suppose they replied that they did, for he then touched off his bombshell, accusing them of having delivered an imperfect ledger, a ledger with the front page missing.

This brought the head stationer round in person calling heaven to witness that when the book left his hands it had been all that a ledger should be, if not more so.

'Somebody must have cut out the page,' he said.

'Absurd!' said the head cashier. 'Nobody but an imbecile would cut out the front page of a ledger.'

'Then,' said the stationer, coming right back at him, 'you must have an imbecile in your department. Have you?'

The head cashier started. This opened up a new line of thought.

'Why, yes,' he admitted, for he was a fair-minded man. 'There is P. G. Wodehouse.'

'Weak in the head, is he, this Wodehouse?'

'Very, so I have always thought.'

'Then send for him and question him narrowly,' said the stationer.

This was done. They got me under the lights and grilled me, and I had to come clean. It was immediately after this that I found myself at liberty, to embark on the life literary.

I

From my earliest years I had always wanted to be a writer. I started turning out the stuff at the age of five. (What I was doing before that, I don't remember. Just loafing, I suppose.)

It was not that I had any particular message for humanity. I am still plugging away and not the ghost of one so far, so it begins to look as though, unless I suddenly hit mid-season form in my eighties, humanity will remain a message short. When I left the bank and turned pro, I just wanted to write, and was prepared to write anything that had a chance of getting into print. And as I surveyed the literary scene, everything looked pretty smooth to me, for the early years of the twentieth century in London – it was in 1902 that the Hong Kong and Shanghai Bank decided (and a very sensible decision, too) that the only way to keep solvent was to de-Wodehouse itself – were not too good for writers at the top of the tree, the big prices being still in the distant future, but they were fine for an industrious young hack who asked no more than to pick up the occasional half-guinea. The dregs, of whom I was one, sat extremely pretty *circa* 1902. There were so many morning papers and evening papers and weekly papers and monthly magazines that you were practically sure of landing your whimsical article on 'The Language of Flowers' or your parody of Omar Khayyám somewhere or other after say thirty-five shots.

I left the bank in September, and by the end of the year found that I had made £65 6s. 7d., so for a beginner I was doing pretty well. But what I needed, to top it off, I felt, was something in the way of a job with a regular salary, and I was fortunate enough to have one fall right into my lap.

There was an evening paper in those days called the *Globe*. It was 105 years old and was printed – so help me – on pink paper. (One of the other evening sheets was printed on green paper. Life was full then, very rich.) It had been a profitable source of income to me for some time because it ran on its front page what were called turnovers, 1000-word articles of almost unparalleled dullness which turned over on to the second page. You dug these out of reference books and got a guinea for them.

In addition to the turnovers the *Globe* carried on its front page a humorous column entitled 'By The Way', and one day I learned that the man who wrote it had been a master at Dulwich when I was there. Sir W. Beach Thomas, no other. These things form a bond. I asked him to work me in as his understudy when he wanted a day off, and he very decently did so, and when he was offered a better job elsewhere, I was taken on permanently. Three guineas a week was the stipend, and it was just what I needed. The work was over by noon, and I had all the rest of the day for freelancing.

What you would call the over-all picture, Winkler, now brightened considerably. There was quite a bit of prestige attached to doing 'By The Way' on the *Globe*. Some well-known writers had done it before Beach Thomas – E. V. Lucas was one of them – and being the man behind the column gave one a certain standing. A parody of Omar Khayyám submitted to a weekly paper – as it might be *Vanity Fair* or *The World* – by P. G. Wodehouse, 'By The Way', the *Globe*, 367 Strand, was much more sympathetically received than would have been a similar effort by P. G. Wodehouse, 21 Walpole Street, Chelsea.

My contributions appeared from time to time in *Punch*, and a couple of times I even got into the *Strand* magazine, which for a young writer in those days was roughly equivalent to being awarded the Order of the Garter. My savings began to mount up. And came a day when I realized that I was sufficiently well fixed to do what I had always dreamed of doing – pay a visit to America.

Why America? I have often wondered about that. Why, I mean, from my earliest years, almost back to the time when I was playing with that orange, was it America that was always to me the land of romance? It is not as though I had been intoxicated by visions of cowboys and Red Indians. Even as a child I never became really cowboy-conscious, and to Red Indians I was definitely allergic, I wanted no piece of them.

And I had no affiliations with the country. My father had spent most of his life in Hong Kong. So had my Uncle Hugh. And two other uncles had been for years in Calcutta and Singapore. You would have expected it to be the Orient that would have called to me. 'Put me somewheres east of Suez,' you would have pictured me saying to myself. But it didn't work out that way. People would see me walking along with a glassy look in my eyes and my mouth hanging open as if I had adenoids and would whisper to one another, 'He's thinking of America.' And they were right.

The *Globe* gave its staff five weeks' holiday in the year. Eight days crossing the Atlantic and eight days crossing it back again was going to abbreviate my visit, but I should at least have nineteen days in New York, so I booked my passage and sailed.

This yearning I had to visit America, rather similar to that of a Tin Pan Alley song-writer longing to get back, back, back to his old Kentucky shack, was due principally, I think, to the fact that I was an enthusiastic boxer in those days and had a boyish reverence for America's pugilists – James J. Corbett, James J. Jeffries, Tom Sharkey, Kid McCoy and the rest of them. I particularly wanted to meet Corbett and shake the hand that had kay-oed John L. Sullivan. I had a letter of introduction to him, but he was in San Francisco when I landed, and I did not get to know him till a good many years later, when he was a charming old gentleman and one of Broadway's leading actors.

But I did meet Kid McCoy. I went out to the camp at White Plains where he was training for his championship fight with Philadelphia Jack O'Brien, and it was at the end of my afternoon there that I made what I can see now – in fact, I saw it almost immediately then – was a rash move. I asked him if I could put on the gloves and have a round with him. I thought it would be something to tell the boys back home, that I had sparred with Kid McCoy.

He assured me he would be delighted, and as we were preparing ourselves for the tourney he suddenly chuckled. He had been reminded, he said, of an entertaining incident in his professional career, when he was fighting a contender who had the misfortune to be stone deaf. It was not immediately that he became aware of the other's affliction, but when he did he acted promptly and shrewdly. As the third round entered its concluding stages he stepped back a pace and pointed to his adversary's corner, to indicate to him that the bell had rung, which of course was not the case but far from it.

'Oh, thank you so much,' said the adversary. 'Very civil of you.'

He dropped his hands and turned away, whereupon Kid McCoy immediately knocked him out.

It was as my host concluded his narrative, laughing heartily at the amusing recollection, that, in Robert Benchley's powerful phrase, I developed a yellow streak which was plainly visible through my clothing. The shape of things to come suddenly took on a most ominous aspect.

'Is this wise, Wodehouse?' I asked myself. 'Is it prudent to go getting yourself mixed up with a middleweight champion of the world whose sense of humour is so strongly marked and so what you might almost describe as warped? Is it not probable that a man with a mind like that will think it droll to knock your fat head off at the roots?'

Very probable indeed, I felt, and that yellow streak began to widen. I debated within myself the idea of calling the whole thing off and making a quick dash for the train. It was an attractive scheme, in which I could see no flaw except that the strategic rearward movement I was planning would put an awful dent in the pride of the Wodehouses. I had never gone much into the family history, but I assumed that my ancestors, like everybody else's, had done well at Crécy and Agincourt, and nobody likes to be a degenerate descendant. I was at a young man's crossroads.

At this moment, as I stood there this way and that dividing the swift mind, like Sir Bedivere, there was a clatter of horse's hooves and a girl came riding up. This was the Kid's wife – he had six of them in an interesting career which ended in a life sentence for murder in Sing-Sing prison – and she caused a welcome diversion. We all became very social, and the McCoy–Wodehouse bout was adjourned *sine die*.

I remember that girl as the prettiest girl I ever saw in my life. Or maybe she just looked good to me at the moment.

## II

Right from the start of my sojourn in New York I don't think I ever had any doubts as to this being the New York of which I had heard so much. 'It looks like New York,' I said to myself as I emerged from the Customs sheds. 'It smells like New York. Yes, I should say it was New York all right.' In which respect I differed completely from Sig. Guiseppe Bartholdi, who, arriving on the plane there from Italy the other day, insisted against all argument that he was in San Francisco.

What happened was that the signor was on his way to visit his son in San Francisco and was not aware of the fact that to get to that city from Italy you have to change at New York and take a westbound plane. All he knew was that his son had told him to come to Montgomery Street, where his – the son's – house was, so when his plane grounded at Idlewild, he hopped out and got into the airport bus, shouting the Italian equivalent of 'California, here I come', and in due course the bus deposited him at the terminus, where he hailed a cab and said 'Montgomery Street, driver, and keep your foot on the accelerator.'

Now it so happens that there is a Montgomery Street in New York, down on the lower east side, and the driver – Jose Navarro of 20 Avenue D., not that it matters – took him there, and pretty soon Sig. Bartholdi, like Othello, was perplexed in the extreme. Nothing the eye could reach resembled the photograph his son had sent him of the house for which he was headed, so he decided to search on foot, and when he had not returned at the end of an hour Mr Navarro drove to the Clinton Street police station and told his story.

About seven p.m. Sig. Bartholdi arrived at the police station escorted by Patrolman J. Aloysius Murphy, and that was where things got complex and etched those deep lines which you can still see on the foreheads of the Clinton Street force. For, as I say, the signor stoutly refused to believe that he was not in San Francisco. Hadn't he seen Montgomery Street with his own eyes? The fact that some men of ill-will had spirited away his son's house had, he said, nothing to do with the case. Either a street is Montgomery Street or it is not Montgomery Street. There is no middle course.

After about forty minutes of this, Mr Patrick Daly, the courteous and popular police lieutenant down Clinton Street way, drew Patrolman Murphy aside. There was a worried expression on his face, and his breathing was rather laboured.

'Look, Aloysius,' he said, 'are you absolutely sure this *is* New York?'

'It's how I always heard the story,' said Patrolman Murphy.

'You have no doubts?'

'Ah, now you're talking, Lieut. If you had asked me that question an hour ago – nay, forty minutes ago – I'd have said "None whatever", but right now I'm beginning to wonder.'

'Me, too. Tell me in your own words, Aloysius, what makes – or shall we say used to make – you think this is New York?'

Patrolman Murphy marshalled his thoughts.

'Well,' he said, 'I live in the Bronx. That's in New York.'

'There may be a Bronx in San Francisco.'

'And here's my badge. Lookut. See what it says on it. "New York City".'

The lieutenant shook his head.

'You can't go by badges. How do we know that some international gang did not steal your San Francisco badge and substitute this one?'

'Would an international gang do that?'

'You never can tell. They're always up to something,' said Lieutenant Daly with a weary sigh.

Well, it all ended happily, I am glad to say. Somebody rang up the signor's son and put the signor on the wire, and the son told him that New York really was New York and that he was to get on the westbound plane at once and come to San Francisco. And there he is now, plumb spang in Montgomery Street, and having a wonderful time. (On a recent picture postcard to a friend in Italy he asserts this in so many words, adding that he wishes he, the friend, were there.) It is a great weight off everybody's mind.

The whole episode has left the Clinton Street personnel a good deal shaken. They are inclined to start at sudden noises and to think that they are being followed about by little men with black beards, and I am not surprised, for they can never tell when something like this may not happen again. And, really, if I were the city of New York, I honestly don't see how I could prove it to a sceptical visitor from Italy. If I were London, yes. That would be simple. I would take the man by the ear and lead him into Trafalgar Square and show him those Landseer lions.

'Look,' I would say. 'Lions. Leeongze. Dash it, man, you know perfectly well that you would never find leeongze like those any-where except in London.'

Upon which the fellow would say, '*Si, si. Grazie,*' and go away with his mind completely set at rest.


III

From 1904 to 1957 is fifty-three years, and I see that you ask in your questionnaire, Winkler, what changes I have noticed in the American scene during that half-century and a bit. Well,

I should say that the principal one is the improvement in American manners.

In 1904 I found residents in the home of the brave and the land of the free, though probably delightful chaps if you got to know them, rather on the brusque side. They shoved you in the street and asked who you were shoving, and used, when spoken to, only one side of the mouth in replying. They were, in a word, pretty tough eggs.

One of my earliest recollections of that first visit of mine to New York is of watching a mob of travellers trying to enter a subway train and getting jammed in the doorway. Two subway officials were standing on the platform, and the first subway official said to the second subway official (speaking out of the starboard side of his mouth), 'Pile 'em in, George!'

Whereupon the two took a running dive at the mass of humanity and started to shove like second-row forwards. It was effective, but it could not happen today. George and his colleague would at least say, 'Pardon us, gentlemen,' before putting their heads down.

For in recent years America has become a nation of Chesterfields, its inhabitants as polite as pallbearers. It may be Emily Post's daily advice on deportment that has brought about this change for the better. Or perhaps it is because I have been over here, setting a good example.

You see it everywhere, this new courtesy.

A waitress in one of the cheaper restaurants on the west side was speaking highly of the polish of a regular customer of hers. 'Every time I serve him anything at the table,' she said, 'he stops eating and raises his hat.'

A man I know was driving in his car the other day and stalled his engine at a street intersection. The lights changed from yellow to green, from green to red, from red to yellow and from yellow to green, but his car remained rooted to the spot. A policeman sauntered up.

'What's the matter, son?' he asked sympathetically. 'Haven't we got any colours you like?'

It is difficult to see how he could have been nicer.

Boxers, too, not so long ago a somewhat uncouth section of the community who were seldom if ever mistaken for members of the Vere de Vere family, have taken on a polish which makes their society a pleasure. They have names like Cyril and Percy and Clarence and live up to them. I can remember the time when, if you asked Kid Biff (the Hoboken Assassin), what in his opinion were his chances in his impending contest with Boko Swat (the Bronx's answer to Civilization), he would reply, 'Dat bum? I'll moider him.' Today it would be, 'The question which you have propounded is by no means an easy one to answer. So many imponderables must be taken into consideration. It is, I mean to say, always difficult to predict before their entry into the arena the outcome of an encounter between two highly trained and skilful welterweights. I may say, however – I am, of course, open to correction – that I am confident of establishing my superiority on the twenty-fourth prox. My manager who, a good deal to my regret, is addicted to the argot, says I'll knock the blighter's block off.'

There was a boxer at the St Nicholas Rink a few weeks ago who came up against an opponent with an unpleasantly forceful left hook which he kept applying to the spot on the athlete's body where, when he was in mufti, his third waistcoat button would have been. His manager watched pallidly from outside the ropes, and when his tiger came back to his corner at the end of the round, was all concern and compassion.

'Joey,' he asked anxiously, 'how do you feel, Joey?'

'Fine, thank you,' said the boxer. 'And you?'

One can almost hear Emily Post cheering in the background.

Even the criminal classes have caught the spirit. From Passaic, New Jersey, comes the news that an unidentified assailant plunged a knife into the shoulder of a Mr James F. Dobson the other day, spun him round and then, seeing his face, clicked his tongue remorsefully.

'Oh, I beg your pardon,' he said. 'I got the wrong guy.'

Frank and manly. If you find yourself in the wrong, admit it and apologize.

Nobody could be more considerate than the modern American. In the Coronet motel outside the town of Danvers, Massachusetts, there is a notice posted asking clients to clean out their rooms before leaving. 'Certainly, certainly, certainly, by all means,' said a recent visitor, and he went off with two table lamps, an inkstand and pen, a mahogany night-table, an ashtray, four sheets, two pillow-cases, two rubber foam pillows, two blankets, two bedspreads, two bath towels, two tumblers and a shower curtain. It was as near to cleaning out the room as he could get, and it must have been saddening to so conscientious a man to be compelled to leave the beds, the mattresses and a twenty-one-inch console television set.

Yes, Manners Makyth Man is the motto of the American of today, though, of course, even today you come across the occasional backslider, the fellow who is not in the movement. A 'slim, elderly man wearing a grey Homburg hat' attracted the notice of the Brooklyn police last week by his habit of going to the turnstile of the Atlantic Avenue subway station, pulling the bar towards him and slipping through the narrow opening, thus getting a free trip, a thing the subway people simply hate.

And what I am leading up to is this. Appearing before Magistrate John R. Starley at the Flatbush Police Court, he continued to wear his Homburg hat. When a court official removed it, he put it on again, and kept putting it on all through the proceedings, though he must have been aware that this is not done. ('Unless you are a private detective, always *always* take your hat off indoors' ... Emily Post.)

It is a pleasure to me to expose this gauche person in print. Michael Rafferty (67) of 812 Myrtle Avenue, Brooklyn. That'll learn you, Mike.

I

Back in London, I found that I had done wisely in going to New York for even so brief a visit. The manner of editors towards me changed. Where before it had been, 'Throw this man out,' they now said, 'Come in, my dear fellow, come in and tell us all about America.' It is hard to believe in these days, when after breakfasting at the Berkeley you nip across the ocean and dine at the Stork Club, but in 1904 anyone in the London writing world who had been to America was regarded with awe and looked upon as an authority on that *terra incognita*. Well, when I tell you that a few weeks after my return *Tit-Bits* was paying me a guinea for an article on New York Crowds and *Sandow's Magazine* 30s. for my description of that happy day at Kid McCoy's training camp, I think I have made my point sufficiently clear.

After that trip to New York I was a man who counted. It was, 'Ask Wodehouse. Wodehouse will know,' when some intricate aspect of American politics had to be explained to the British public. My income rose like a rocketing pheasant. I made £505 1s. 7d. in 1906 and £527 17s. 1d. in 1907 and was living, I suppose, on about £203 4s. 9d. In fact, if on November 17th, 1907, I had not bought a secondhand Darracq car for £450 (and smashed it up in the first week) I should soon have been one of those economic royalists who get themselves so disliked. This unfortunate venture brought my capital back to about where it had started, and a long and dusty road had to be travelled before my finances were in a state sufficiently sound to justify another visit to America.

I was able to manage it in the spring of 1909.

## II

At the time of this second trip to New York I was still on the *Globe* doing the 'By The Way' column, and had come over anticipating that after nineteen days I would have to tear myself away with many a longing lingering look behind and go back to the salt mines. But on the sixth day a strange thing happened. I had brought with me a couple of short stories, and I sold one of them to the *Cosmopolitan* and the other to *Collier's* for $200 and $300 respectively, both on the same morning. That was at that time roughly £40 and £60, and to one like myself whose highest price for similar bijoux had been ten guineas a throw, the discovery that American editors were prepared to pay on this stupendous scale was like suddenly finding a rich uncle from Australia. This, I said to myself, is the place for me.

I realized, of course, that New York was more expensive than London, but even so one could surely live there practically for ever on $500. Especially as there were always the good old *Cosmopolitan* and jolly old *Collier's* standing by with their cornucopias, all ready to start pouring. To seize pen and paper and post my resignation to the *Globe* was with me the work of an instant. Then, bubbling over with hope and ambition, I took a room at the Hotel Duke down in Greenwich Village and settled in with a secondhand typewriter, paper, pencils, envelopes and Bartlett's book of *Familiar Quotations*, that indispensable adjunct to literary success.

I wonder if Bartlett has been as good a friend to other authors as he has been to me. I don't know where I would have been all these years without him. It so happens that I am not very bright and find it hard to think up anything really clever off my own bat, but give me my Bartlett and I will slay you.

It has always been a puzzle to me how Bartlett did it, how he managed to compile a volume of 3 million quotations or whatever it is. One can see, of course, how he started. I picture him at a loose end one morning, going about shuffling his feet and whistling and kicking stones, and his mother looked out of the window and said, 'John, dear, I wish you wouldn't fidget like that. Why don't you find something to *do*?'

'Such as...?' said John Bartlett (born at Plymouth, Mass., in 1820).

'Dig in the garden.'

'Don't want to dig in the garden.'

'Or spin your top.'

'Don't *want* to spin my top.'

'Then why not compile a book of familiar quotations, a collection of passages, phrases and proverbs, traced to their sources in ancient and modern literature?'

John Bartlett's face lit up. He lost that sullen look.

'Mater,' he said, 'I believe you've got something there. I see what you mean. "To be or not to be" and all that guff. I'll start right away. Paper!' said John Bartlett. 'Lots of paper, and can anyone lend me a pencil?'

So far, so good. But after that what? One cannot believe that he had all literature at his fingers' ends and knew just what Aldus Manutius said in 1472 and Narcisse Achille, Comte de Salvandy, in 1797. I suppose he went about asking people.

'Know anything good?' he would say, button-holing an acquaintance.

'Shakespeare?'

'No, I've got Shakespeare.'

'How about Pliny the Younger?'

'Never heard of him, but shoot.'

'Pliny the Younger said, "Objects which are usually the motives of our travels by land and by sea are often overlooked if they lie under our eye."'

'He called that hot, did he?' says John Bartlett with an ugly sneer.

The acquaintance stiffens.

'If it was good enough for Pliny the Younger it ought to be good enough for a pop-eyed young pipsqueak born at Plymouth, Mass., in 1820.'

'All right, all right, no need to get steamed up about it. How are you on Pliny the Elder?'

'Pliny the Elder said "Everything is soothed by oil."'

'Everything is what by *what*?'

'Soothed by oil.'

'How about sardines?' says John Bartlett with a light laugh. 'Well, all right, I'll bung it down, but I don't think much of it.'

And so the book got written. In its original form it contained only 295 pages, but the latest edition runs to 1254, not counting 577 pages of index, and one rather unpleasant result of this continual bulging process is that Bartlett today has become frightfully mixed. It is like a conservative old club that has had to let down the barriers and let in a whole lot of rowdy young new members to lower the tone. There was a time when you couldn't get elected to Bartlett unless you were Richard Bethell, Lord Westbury (1800–73) or somebody like that, but now you never know who is going to pop out at you from its pages. Gabriel Romanovitch Dershavin (1743–1816) often says to Alexis Charles Henri Clerel de Tocqueville (1805–59) that it gives him a pain in the neck.

'Heaven knows I'm no snob,' he says, 'but really when it comes to being expected to mix with non-U outsiders like P. G. Wodehouse and the fellow who wrote *The Man Who Broke the Bank at Monte Carlo*, well, dash it!'

And Alexis Charles Henri says he knows exactly how Gabriel Romanovitch feels, and he has often felt the same way himself. They confess themselves at a loss to imagine what the world is coming to.

Nevertheless and be that as it may, Bartlett, with all thy faults we love thee still. How many an erudite little article of mine would not have been written without your never-failing sympathy, encouragement, and advice. So all together, boys.

'What's the matter with Bartlett?'

'He's all right!'

'Who's all right?'

'Bartlett! Bartlett! Bartlett! For he's a jolly good fellow, for he's a jolly good fellow, for he's a jolly good fe-hel-low....'

And no heel-taps.

## III

I was down having a nostalgic look at the Hotel Duke the other day, and was shocked to find that in the forty-seven years during which I had taken my eye off it it had blossomed out into no end of a high-class joint with a Champagne Room or a Diamond Horseshoe or something like that, where you can dance nightly to the strains of somebody's marimba band. In 1909 it was a seedy rookery inhabited by a group of young writers as impecunious as myself, who had no time or inclination for dancing. We paid weekly (meals included) about what you tip the waiter nowadays after a dinner for two, and it was lucky for me that the management did not charge more. If they had, I should have been in the red at the end of the first few months.

For it was not long before I made the unpleasant discovery that though I had a certain facility for dialogue and a nice light comedy touch – at least, I thought it was nice – my output was not everybody's dish. After that promising start both *Collier's* and the *Cosmopolitan* weakened and lost their grip. If it had not been for the pulps – God bless them – I should soon have been looking like a famine victim.

I have written elsewhere – in a book called *Heavy Weather*, if you don't mind me slipping in a quick advert – that the ideal towards which the City Fathers of all English country towns strive is to provide a public house for each individual inhabitant. It was much the same in New York in 1909 as regards the pulp magazines. There was practically one per person. They flooded the bookstalls, and it was entirely owing to them that I was able in those days to obtain the calories without which it is fruitless to try to keep the roses in the cheeks.

Not that I obtained such a frightful lot of calories, for there was nothing of the lavishness of *Collier's* and *Cosmopolitan* about the pulps. They believed in austerity for their contributors, and one was lucky to get $50 for a story. Still, $50 here and $50 there helps things along, and I was able to pay my weekly bill at the

Duke and sometimes – very occasionally – to lunch at a good restaurant. And after a year or so a magazine called *Vanity Fair* was started and I was taken on as its dramatic critic.

I blush a little as I make that confession, for I know where dramatic critics rank in the social scale. Nobody loves them, and rightly, for they are creatures of the night. Has anybody ever seen a dramatic critic in the daytime? I doubt it. They come out after dark, and we know how we feel about things that come out after dark. Up to no good, we say to ourselves.

Representing a monthly magazine, I was excluded from the opening performance and got my seats on the second night. This of course was rather humiliating and made me feel I was not really a force, but I escaped the worries that beset the dramatic critic of a morning paper. The inkstained wretches who cover the new plays for the dailies have a tough assignment. Having to rush off to the office and get their notice in by midnight, every minute counts with them, and too often they find themselves on a first night barred from the exit door by a wall of humanity.

The great thing, according to John McLain of the *NY Journal-American*, is to beat the gun, and with this in mind he employs two methods. One is to keep his eye on the curtain, and the minute it starts to quiver at the top, showing that the evening's entertainment is about to conclude, to be off up the aisle like a jack-rabbit. The other is to anticipate the curtain line, but here too often the dramatist fools you. At a recent opening the heroine, taking the centre of the stage at about five minutes to eleven, passed a weary hand over her brow and whispered, 'And that . . . is all.' That seemed good enough to Mr McLain and he was out of the theatre in a whirl of dust, little knowing that after his departure the hero entered (l.) and said, 'All what?' and the play went on for another half-hour.

Having two weeks in which to write my critique, I missed all that.

So what with my $50 here and my $50 there and my salary from *Vanity Fair*, I was making out fairly well. All right so far, about summed it up.

But I was not satisfied. I wanted something much more on the order of a success story, and I would be deceiving your newspaper and radio public, Winkler, if I were to say I did not chafe. I chafed very frequently.

You know how it is, J.P. You ask yourself what you are doing with this life of yours, and it is galling to have to answer, 'Well, if you must pin me down, not such a frightful lot.' It seemed to me that the time had arrived to analyse and evaluate my position with a view to taking steps through the proper channels. I was particularly anxious to put my finger on the reason why slick-paper magazines like the *Saturday Evening Post* did not appear to want their Wodehouse.

Quite suddenly I spotted what the trouble was. It came to me like a flash one day when I was lunching on a ham sandwich (with dill pickle) and a glass of milk.

My name was all wrong.

This matter of names is of vital importance to those who practise the Arts. There is nothing about which they have to be more careful. Consider the case of Frank Lovejoy, the movie star, who for a time was not getting anywhere in his profession and couldn't think why till one morning his agent explained it to him.

'We meet producer resistance,' the agent told him, 'on account of your name. The studio heads don't think Frank Lovejoy a suitable name for a movie star. You'll have to change it. What they want today is *strong* names, like Rock Hudson, Tab Hunter and so on. Try to think of something.'

'Stab Zanuch?'

'Not bad.'

'Or Max Million?'

'Better still. That's got it.'

But a week later Mr Lovejoy had a telephone call from his agent.

'Max Million speaking,' he said.

'It is, is it? Well, it better not be,' said the agent. 'The trend has changed. They don't want strong names any more, they want *sincere* names.'

'How do you mean, sincere names?'

'Well, like Abe Lincoln.'

'Abe Washington?'

'Abe Washington is fine.'

'Or Ike Franklin?'

'No, I think Abe Washington's better.'

For some days Abe Washington went about feeling that prosperity was just around the corner, and then the telephone rang once more.

'Sorry, kid,' said the agent, 'but the trend has changed again. They want *geographical* names, like John Ireland.'

So Frank Lovejoy became George Sweden, and all seemed well, with the sun smiling through and all that sort of thing, but his contentment was short-lived. The agent rang up to say that there had been another shift in the party line and the trend was now towards *familiar* names like Gary Stewart, Clark Cooper and Alan Gable. So Frank Lovejoy became Marlon Ladd and might be so to this day, had not he had another call from the agent.

'There's been a further shake-up,' the agent said. 'What they want now are *happy* names suggestive of love and joy.'

'How about Frank Lovejoy?'

'Swell,' said the agent.

But I was telling you about my name being wrong. All this while, you see, I had been labelling my stories

BY

P. G. WODEHOUSE

and at this time when a writer for the American market who went about without three names was practically going around naked. Those were the days of Richard Harding Davis, of Margaret Culkin Banning, of James Warner Bellah, of Earl Derr Biggers, of Charles Francis Coe, Norman Reilly Raine, Mary Roberts Rinehart, Clarence Budington Kelland and Orison Swett – yes, really, I'm not kidding – Marden. And here was I, poor misguided simp, trying to get by with a couple of contemptible initials.

No wonder the slicks would not take my work. In anything like a decent magazine I would have stood out as conspicuously as a man in a sweater and cap at the Eton and Harrow match.

It frequently happens that when you get an inspiration, you don't stop there but go right ahead and get another. My handicap when starting to write for American editors had always been that I knew so little of American life, and it now occurred to me that I had not yet tried them with anything about English life. I knew quite a lot about what went on in English country houses with their earls and butlers and younger sons. In my childhood in Worcestershire and later in my Shropshire days I had met earls and butlers and younger sons in some profusion, and it was quite possible, it now struck me, that the slick magazines would like to read about them.

I had a plot all ready and waiting, and two days later I was typing on a clean white page

## SOMETHING FRESH
### BY
### PELHAM GRENVILLE WODEHOUSE

and I had a feeling that I was going to hit the jackpot. It seemed incredible to me that all this time, like the base Indian who threw away a pearl richer than all his tribe, I should have been failing to cash in on such an income-producing combination as Pelham Grenville Wodehouse. It put me right up there with Harry Leon Wilson, David Graham Phillips, Arthur Somers Roche and Hugh McNair Kahler.

If you ask me to tell you frankly if I like the name Pelham Grenville Wodehouse, I must confess that I do not. I have my dark moods when it seems to me about as low as you can get. I was named after a godfather, and not a thing to show for it but a small silver mug which I lost in 1897. But I was born at a time when children came to the font not knowing what might not happen to them before they were dried off and taken home. My three brothers were christened respectively Philip Peveril, Ernest Armine and Lancelot Deane, so I was probably lucky not to get something wished on me like Hyacinth Augustus or Albert Prince Consort. And say what you will of Pelham Grenville, shudder though you may at it, it changed the luck. *Something Fresh* was bought as a serial by the *Saturday Evening Post* for what *Variety* would call a hotsy $3500. It was the first of the series which I may call the Blandings Castle saga, featuring Clarence, ninth Earl of Emsworth, his pig Empress of Blandings, his son the Hon. Freddie Threepwood and his butler Beach, concerning whom I have since written so much.

## IV

Too much, carpers have said. So have cavillers. They see these
chronicles multiplying like rabbits down the years and the prospect appals them. Only the other day a critic, with whose name
I will not sully my typewriter, was giving me the sleeve across
the windpipe for this tendency of mine to write so much about
members of the British peerage. Specifically, he accused me of
an undue fondness of earls.

Well, of course, now that I come to tot up the score, I do
realize that in the course of my literary career I have featured
quite a number of these fauna, but as I often say – well, perhaps
once a fortnight – why not? I see no objection to earls. A most
respectable class of men they seem to me. And one admires their
spirit. I mean, while some, of course, have come up the easy way,
many have had the dickens of a struggle, starting at the bottom
of the ladder as mere Hons., having to go into dinner after the
Vice-Chancellor of the Duchy of Lancaster and all that sort of
thing. Show me the Hon. who by pluck and determination has
raised himself step by step from the depths till he has become
entitled to keep a coronet on the hat-peg in the downstairs cup-
board, and I will show you a man of whom any author might be
proud to write.

Earls on the whole have made a very good showing in fiction.
With baronets setting them a bad example by being almost uniformly steeped in crime, they have preserved a gratifyingly high
standard of behaviour. There is seldom anything wrong with the
earl in fiction, if you don't mind a touch of haughtiness and a
tendency to have heavy eyebrows and draw them together in a
formidable frown. And in real life I can think of almost no earls
whose hearts were not as pure and fair as those of dwellers in the

lowlier air of Seven Dials. I would trust the average earl as implicitly as I trust bass singers, and I can't say more than that. I should like to digress for a moment on the subject of bass singers.

What splendid fellows they are, are they not? I would think twice before putting my confidence in the tenor who makes noises like gas escaping from a pipe, and baritones are not much better, but when a man brings it up from the soles of his feet, very loud and deep and manly, you know instinctively that his heart is in the right place. Anyone who has ever heard the curate at a village concert rendering 'Old Man River', particularly the 'He don't plant taters, he don't plant cotton' passage, with that odd effect of thunder rumbling in the distance, has little doubt that his spiritual needs are in safe hands.

Am I right in thinking that nowadays the supply of bass singers is giving out? At any rate, it is only rarely today that a bass singer gets a song to himself. As a general rule he is just a man with a side shirt-front who stands on one side and goes 'Zim-zim-zim' while the tenor is behaving like Shelley's skylark. It was not like this in the good old days. When I was a boy, no village concert was complete without the item:

6. Song: 'Asleep on the Deep' (Rev. Hubert Voules)

while if one went to a music-hall one was always confronted at about ten o'clock by a stout man in baggy evening dress with a diamond solitaire in his shirt-front, who walked on the stage in a resolute way and stood glaring at you with one hand in the armhole of his waistcoat.

You knew he was not a juggler or a conjurer, because he had no props and no female assistant in pink tights. And you knew he was not a dramatic twenty-minute sketch, because he would have had a gag along with him. And presently you had him tabbed. He was a – bass, naturally – patriotic singer, and he sang a song with some such refrain as:

> For England's England still.
> It is, and always will.
> Though foreign foes may brag,
> We love our dear old flag,
> And old Enger-land is Enger-land still.

But where is he now? And where is the curate with his 'Asleep on the Deep' (going right down into the cellar on that 'So beware, so beware' line)?

This gradual fading-out of the bass singer is due, I should imagine, to the occupational hazards inseparable from his line of work. When a bass singer finds that night after night he gets his chin caught in his collar or – on the deeper notes – makes his nose bleed, he becomes dispirited. 'Surely,' he says to himself, 'there must be other, less risky ways of entertaining one's public', and the next time you see him he has taken to card tricks or imitations of feathered songsters who are familiar to you all. Or, as I say, he just stands in the background going 'Zim-zim-zim' – this is fairly free from danger – and leaves the prizes of the profession to the sort of man who sings 'Trees' in a reedy falsetto.

I was very touched the other day when I read in one of the papers the following item:

Montgomery, Alabama. Orville P. Gray, twenty-seven-year-old bass singer serving a sentence at Kilby prison, has turned down a chance for parole. Gray told Parole Supervisor E. M. Parkman that he does not want to break up the prison quartette, of which he is a member.

Would you get a tenor making that supreme sacrifice? Or a baritone? Not in a million years. It takes a man who can reach down into the recesses of his socks and come up with

> He must know sumfin', he don't say nuffin',
> He just keeps rollin' along

to do the square thing, with no thought of self, on such a majestic scale.

But to get back to earls (many of whom, I have no doubt, sing bass). They are, as I was saying, fine fellows all of them, not only in real life but on the printed page. English literature, lacking them, would have been a good deal poorer. Shakespeare would have been lost without them. Everyone who has written for the theatre knows how difficult it is to get people off the stage unless you can think of a good exit speech for them. Shakespeare had no such problem. With more earls at his disposal than he knew what to do with he was on velvet. One need only quote those well-known lines from his *Henry VII, Part Two*:

> My lord of Sydenham, bear our royal word
> To Brixton's earl, the Earl of Wormwood Scrubbs,
> Our faithful liege, the Earl of Dulwich (East),
> And those of Beckenham, Penge and Peckham Rye,
> Together with the Earl of Hampton Wick
> Bid them to haste like cats when struck with brick,
> For they are needed in our battle line,
> And stitch in time doth ever save full nine.
>
> (Exeunt Omnes. Trumpets and hautboys.)

'Pie!' Shakespeare used to say to Burbage, and Burbage would agree that Shakespeare earned his money easily.

A thing about earls I have never understood, and never liked to ask anyone for fear of betraying my ignorance, is why one earl is the Earl of Whoosis and another earl just Earl Smith. I have an idea – I may be wrong – that the 'of' boys have a social edge on the others, like the aristocrats in Germany who are able to call themselves 'Von'. One can picture the Earl of Berkeley Square being introduced to Earl Piccadilly at a cocktail-party.

The host says, 'Oh, Percy, I want you to meet Earl Piccadilly,' and hurries off to attend to his other guests. There is a brief interval during which the two agree that this is the rottenest party they were ever at and that the duke, their host, is beginning to show his age terribly, then the Earl of Berkeley Square says: 'I didn't quite get the name. Earl of Piccadilly, did he say?'

'No, just Earl Piccadilly.'

The Earl of Berkeley Square starts. A coldness creeps into his manner. He looks like Nancy Mitford hearing the word 'serviette' mentioned in her presence.

'You mean *plain* Earl Piccadilly?'

'That's right.'

'No "of"?'

'No, no "of".'

There is a tense silence. You can see the Earl of Berkeley Square's lip curling. At a house like the duke's he had not expected to have to hobnob with the proletariat.

'Ah, well,' he says at length with a nasty little snigger, 'it takes all sorts to make a world, does it not?' and Earl Piccadilly slinks off with his ears pinned back and drinks far too many sherries in the hope of restoring his self-respect.

Practically all the earls who are thrown sobbing out of cocktail-parties are non-ofs. They can't take it, poor devils.

NOTE. (Not a footnote, just a note.) A friend, to whom I showed the manuscript of this book, does not see altogether eye to eye with me in my eulogy of bass singers. You get, he reminded me, some very dubious characters who sing bass. Mephistopheles in *Faust*, for one. Would you, he said, trust Mephistopheles with your wallet? And how about Demon Kings in pantomime?

There is, I must admit, a certain amount of truth in this. I don't suppose there is a man much lower in the social scale than the typical Demon King. Not only does he never stop plotting against the welfare of the principal boy and girl, but he goes in for loud spangles and paints his face green, thus making himself look like a dissipated lizard. Many good judges claim that he is the worst thing that has happened to England since the top hat. And yet he unquestionably sings bass. One can only assume that he is a bass singer who went wrong in early youth through mixing with bad companions.

I

The same critic who charged me with stressing the Earl note too determinedly in my writings also said that I wrote far too much about butlers.

How do you feel about that, Winkler? Do you think I do? There may be something in it, of course.

The fact is, butlers have always fascinated me. As a child, I lived on the fringe of the butler belt. As a young man, I was a prominent pest at houses where butlers were maintained. And later I employed butlers. So it might be said that I have never gone off the butler standard. For fifty years I have omitted no word or act to keep these supermen in the forefront of public thought, and now – with all these social revolutions and what not – they have ceased to be.

I once read an arresting story about a millionaire whose life was darkened by a shortage of pigeons. He had the stuff in sack-fuls, but no pigeons. Or, rather, none of the particular breed he wanted. In his boyhood these birds had been plentiful, but now all his vast wealth could not procure a single specimen, and this embittered him. 'Oh, bring back my pigeon to me!' was his cry. I am feeling these days just as he did. I can do without pigeons – Walter Pidgeon always excepted, of course – but it does break me up to think that I have been goggled at by my last butler.

It is possible that at this point, J.P., you will try to cheer me up by mentioning a recent case in the London courts where a young peer was charged with biting a lady friend in the leg and much of the evidence was supplied by 'the butler'. I read about that, too, and it did cheer me up for a moment. But only for a moment. All too soon I was telling myself cynically that this 'butler' was probably merely another of these modern make-shifts. No doubt in many English homes there is still buttling of a sort going on, but it is done by ex-batmen, promoted odd-job boys and the like, callow youngsters not to be ranked as butlers by one who, like myself, was around and about in the London of 1903, and saw the real thing. Butlers? A pack of crude young amateurs without a double chin among them? Faugh, if you will permit me the expression.

A man I know has a butler, and I was congratulating him on this the last time we met. He listened to me, I thought, rather moodily.

'Yes,' he said when I had finished, 'Murgatroyd is all right, I suppose. Does his work well and all that sort of thing. But,' he added with a sigh, 'I wish I could break him of that habit of his of sliding down the banisters.'

The real crusted, vintage butler passed away with Edward the Seventh. One tried one's best to pretend that the Georgian Age had changed nothing, but it had. The post-First World War butler was a mere synthetic substitute for the ones we used to know. When we septuagenarians speak of butlers, we are think-ing of what used to lurk behind the front doors of Mayfair at the turn of the century.

Those were the days of what – because they took place late in the afternoon – were known as morning calls. Somewhere around five o'clock one would put on the old frock-coat (with the white piping at the edge of the waistcoat), polish up the old top hat (a drop of stout helped the gloss), slide a glove over one's left hand (you carried the other one) and go out and pay morning calls. You mounted the steps of some stately home, you pulled the bell, and suddenly the door opened and there stood an august figure, weighing seventeen stone or so on the hoof, with mauve cheeks, three chins, supercilious lips and bulging gooseberry eyes that raked you with a forbidding stare as if you were something the carrion crow had deposited on the doorstep. 'Not at all what we have been accustomed to,' those eyes seemed to say.

That, at least, was the message I always read in them, owing no doubt to my extreme youth and the fact, of which I never ceased to be vividly aware, that my brother Armine's frock-coat and my cousin George's trousers did not begin to fit me. A certain anaemia of the exchequer caused me in those days to go about in the discarded clothes of relatives, and it was this that once enabled me to see that rarest of all sights, a laughing butler. (By the laws of their guild, butlers of the Edwardian epoch were sometimes permitted a quick, short smile, provided it was sardonic, but never a guffaw. I will come back to this later. Wait for the story of the laughing butler.)

My acquaintance with butlers and my awe of them started at a very early age. My parents were in Hong Kong most of the time when I was in the knickerbocker stage, and during my school holidays I was passed from aunt to aunt. A certain number of these aunts were the wives of clergymen, which meant official calls at the local great house, and when they paid these calls they took me along. Why, I have never been able to understand, for even at the age of ten I was a social bust, contributing little or nothing to the feast of reason and flow of soul beyond shuffling my feet and kicking the leg of the chair into which loving hands had dumped me. There always came a moment when my hostess, smiling one of those painful smiles, suggested that it would be nice for your little nephew to go and have tea in the servants' hall.

And she was right. I loved it. My mind today is fragrant with memories of kindly footmen and vivacious parlour-maids. In their society I forgot to be shy and kidded back and forth with the best of them. The life and the soul of the party, they probably described me as, if they ever wrote their reminiscences.

But these good times never lasted. Sooner or later in would come the butler, like the monstrous crow in *Through The Looking Glass*, and the quips would die on our lips. 'The young gentleman is wanted,' he would say morosely, and the young gentleman would shamble out, feeling like 30¢.

Butlers in those days, when they retired, married the cook and went and let lodgings to hard-up young men in Ebury Street and the King's Road, Chelsea, so, grown to man's estate, I found myself once more in contact with them. But we never at that time became intimate. Occasionally, in a dare-devil mood, encountering my landlord in the street, I would say, 'Good morning, Mr Briggs' or Biggs, or whatever it might be, but the coldness of his 'Good morning, sir' told me that he desired no advances from one so baggy at the trouser-knee as myself, and our relations continued distant. It was only in what my biographers will speak of as my second London period – *circa* 1930 – when I was in the chips and an employer of butlers, that I came to know them well and receive their confidences.

By that time I had reached the age when the hair whitens, the waistline expands and the terrors of youth leave us. The turning point came when I realized one morning that, while I was on the verge of fifty, my butler was a Johnny-come-lately of forty-six.

It altered the whole situation. One likes to unbend with the youngsters, and I unbent with this slip of a boy. From tentative discussions of the weather we progressed until I was telling him what hell it was to get stuck half-way through a novel, and he was telling me of former employers of his and how the thing that sours butlers is having to stand behind their employer's chair at dinner night after weary night and listen to the funny noise he makes when drinking soup. You serve the soup and stand back and clench your hands. 'Now comes the funny noise,' you say to yourself. Night after night after night. This explains what in my youth had always puzzled me, the universal gloom of butlers.

Only once – here comes that story I was speaking of – have I heard a butler laugh. On a certain night in the year 1903 I had been invited to dinner at a rather more stately home than usual and, owing to the friend who has appeared in some of my stories under the name of Ukridge having borrowed my dress clothes without telling me, I had to attend the function in a primitive suit of soup-and-fish bequeathed to me by my Uncle Hugh, a man who stood six feet four and weighed in the neighbourhood of fifteen stone.

Even as I dressed, the things seemed roomy. It was not, how-ever, until the fish course that I realized how roomy they were, when, glancing down, I suddenly observed the trousers mount-ing like a rising tide over my shirt-front. I pushed them back, but I knew I was fighting a losing battle. I was up against the same trouble that bothered King Canute. Eventually when I was helping myself to potatoes and was off my guard, the tide swept up as far as my white tie, and it was then that Yates or Bates or Fotheringay or whatever his name was uttered a sound like a bursting paper bag and hurried from the room with his hand over his mouth, squaring himself with his guild later, I believe, by saying he had had some kind of fit. It was an unpleasant experience and one that clouded my life through most of the period 1903-4-5, but it is something to be able to tell my grandchildren that I once saw a butler laugh.

Among other things which contributed to make butlers gloomy was the fact that so many of their employers were sparkling raconteurs. Only a butler, my butler said, can realize what it means to a butler to be wedged against the sideboard, unable to escape, and to hear his employer working the conversation round to the point where he will be able to tell that good story of his which he, the butler, has heard so often before. It was when my butler mentioned this, with a kindly word of commendation to me for never having said anything even remotely clever or entertaining since he had entered my service, that I at last found myself understanding the inwardness of a rather peculiar episode of my early manhood.

A mutual friend had taken me to lunch at the house of W. S. (Savoy Operas) Gilbert, and midway through the meal the great man began to tell a story. It was one of those very long deceptively dull stories where you make the build-up as tedious as you can, knowing that the punch line is going to pay for everything, and pause before you reach the point so as to stun the audience with the unexpected snaperoo. In other words, a story which is pretty awful till the last line, when you have them rolling in the aisles.

Well, J.P., there was Sir William Schwenk Gilbert telling this long story, and there was I, tucked away inside my brother Armine's frock-coat and my cousin George's trousers, drinking it respectfully in. It did not seem to me a very funny story, but I knew it must be because this was W. S. Gilbert telling it, so when the pause before the punch line came, thinking that this was the end, I laughed.

I had rather an individual laugh in those days, something like the explosion of one of those gas mains that slay six. Infectious, I suppose you would call it, for the other guests, seeming a little puzzled, as if they had expected something better from the author of *The Mikado*, all laughed politely, and conversation became general. And it was at this juncture that I caught my host's eye.

I shall always remember the glare of pure hatred which I saw in it. If you have seen photographs of Gilbert, you will be aware that even when in repose his face was inclined to be formidable and his eye not the sort of eye you would willingly catch. And now his face was far from being in repose. His eyes, beneath their beetling brows, seared my very soul. In order to get away from them, I averted my gaze and found myself encountering that of the butler. His eyes were shining with a doglike devotion. For some reason which I was unable to understand, I appeared to have made his day. I know now what the reason was. I suppose he had heard that story build up like a glacier and rumble to its conclusion at least fifty times, probably more, and I had killed it.

And now, Gilbert has gone to his rest, and his butler has gone to his rest, and all the other butlers of those great days have gone to their rests. Time, like an ever-rolling stream, bears all its sons away, and even the Edwardian butler has not been immune. He has joined the Great Auk, Mah Jong and the snows of yesterday in limbo.

But I like to think that this separation of butler and butler-*aficionado* will not endure for ever. I tell myself that when Clarence, ninth Earl of Emsworth, finally hands in his dinner pail after his long and pleasant life, the first thing he will hear as he settles himself on his cloud will be the fruity voice of Beach, his faithful butler, saying, 'Nectar or ambrosia, m'lord?'

'Eh? Oh, hullo, Beach. I say, Beach, what's this dashed thing they handed me as I came in?'

'A harp, m'lord. Your lordship is supposed to play on it.'

'Eh? Play on it? Like Harpo Marx, you mean?'

'Precisely, m'lord.'

'Most extraordinary. Is everybody doing it?'

'Yes, m'lord.'

'My sister Constance? My brother Galahad? Sir Gregory Parsloe? Baxter? Everybody?'

'Yes, m'lord.'

'Well, it all sounds very odd to me. Still, if you say so. Give me your A, Beach.'

'Certainly, m'lord. Coming right up.'

I

Those stray thoughts on earls and butlers which I have just recorded were written as a dignified retort to a critic dissatisfied with the pearls which I had cast before him, and I see, Winkler, referring to your questionnaire, that you want to know if I am influenced by criticisms of my work.

That, I suppose, depends on whether those who criticize my work are good or bad critics. A typical instance of the bad critic is the one who said, 'It is time that Mr Wodehouse realized that Jeeves has become a bore.' When my press-cutting bureau sends me something like that, an icy look comes into my hard grey eyes and I mark my displeasure by not pasting it into my scrapbook. Let us forget this type of man and turn to the rare souls who can spot a good thing when they see one, and shining like a beacon among these is the woman who wrote to the daily paper the other day to say that she considers Shakespeare 'grossly materialistic and much overrated' and 'greatly prefers P. G. Wodehouse'.

Well, it is not for me to say whether she is right or not. One cannot arbitrate in these matters of taste. Shakespeare's stuff is different from mine, but that is not necessarily to say that it is inferior. There are passages in Shakespeare to which I would have been quite pleased to put my name. That 'Tomorrow and tomorrow and tomorrow' thing. Some spin on the ball there. I doubt, too, if I have ever done anything much better than Falstaff. The man may have been grossly materialistic, but he could crack them through the covers all right when he got his eye in. I would place him definitely in the Wodehouse class.

One of the things people should remember when they compare Shakespeare with me and hand him the short straw is that he did not have my advantages. I have privacy for my work, he had none. When I write a novel I sit down and write it. I may have to break off from time to time to get up and let the foxhound out and let the foxhound in, and let the cat out and let the cat in, and let the senior Peke out and let the senior Peke in, and let the junior Peke out and let the junior Peke in, and let the cat out again, but nobody interrupts me, nobody comes breathing down the back of my neck and asks me how I am getting on. Shakespeare, on the other hand, never had a moment to himself.

Burbage, I imagine, was his worst handicap. Even today a dramatic author suffers from managers, but in Shakespeare's time anybody who got mixed up in the theatre was like somebody in a slave camp. The management never let him alone. In those days a good run for a play was one night. Anything over that was sensational. Shakespeare, accordingly, would dash off *Romeo and Juliet* for production on Monday, and on Tuesday morning at six o'clock round would come Burbage in a great state of excitement and wake him with a wet sponge.

'Asleep!' Burbage would say, seeming to address an invisible friend on whose sympathy he knew he could rely. 'Six o'clock in the morning and still wallowing in hoggish slumber! Is this a system? Don't I get no service and co-operation? Good heavens, Will, why aren't you working?'

Shakespeare sits up and rubs his eyes.

'Oh, hullo, Burb. That you? How are the notices?'

'Never mind the notices. Don't you realize we've gotta give 'em something tomorrow?'

'What about *Romeo and Juliet*?'

'Came off last night. How long do you expect these charades to run? If you haven't something to follow, we'll have to close the theatre. Got anything?'

'Not a thing.'

'Then what do you suggest?'

'Bring on the bears.'

'They don't want bears, they want a play, and stop groaning like that. Groaning won't get us anywhere.'

So Shakespeare would heave himself out of bed, and by lunchtime, with Burbage popping in and out with his eternal 'How ya gettin' on?' he would somehow manage to write *Othello*. And Burbage would skim through it and say, 'It'll need work,' but he supposed it would have to do.

An author cannot give of his best under these conditions, and this, I think, accounts for a peculiarity in Shakespeare's output which has escaped the notice of the critics – to wit, the fact that while what he turns out sounds all right, it generally doesn't mean anything. There can be little doubt that when he was pushed for time – as when was he not? – William Shakespeare just shoved down anything and trusted to the charity of the audience to pull him through.

'What on earth does "abroach" mean, laddie?' Burbage would ask, halting the rehearsal of *Romeo and Juliet*.

'It's something girls wear,' Shakespeare would say. 'You know. Made of diamonds and fastened with a pin.'

'But you've got in the script, "Who set this ancient quarrel new abroach?" and it doesn't seem to make sense.'

'Oh, it's all in the acting,' Shakespeare would say. 'Just speak the line quick and nobody'll notice anything.'

And that would be that, till they were putting on *Pericles, Prince of Tyre*, and somebody had to say to somebody else, 'I'll fetch thee with a wanion.' Shakespeare would get round that by pretending that a wanion was the latest court slang for cab, but this gave him only a brief respite, for the next moment they would be asking him what a 'geck' was, or a 'loggat', or a 'cullion' or an 'egma' or a 'punto' and wanting to know what he meant by saying a character had become 'frampold' because he was 'rawly'.

It was a wearing life, and though Shakespeare would try to pass it off jocularly by telling the boys at the Mermaid that it was all in a lifetime and the first hundred years were the hardest and all that sort of thing, there can be little doubt that he felt the strain and that it affected the quality of his work.

So I think the woman who wrote to the paper ought to try to be kinder to Shakespeare. Still, awfully glad you like my stuff, old thing, and I hope you don't just get it out of the library. Even if you do, 'At-a-girl, and cheers.'

II

This episode had rather an unpleasant sequel. A letter was forwarded to me from the paper – addressed to the editor and signed 'Indignant' – which began:

Sir – I was completely confounded to read in this morning's —— the statement by your correspondent 'Highland Lassie' that P. G. Wodehouse is a better writer than Shakespeare. As an authority on the latter I can definitely state he was the greatest genius of his time, to be compared only with Riley, Drake and Nelson.

These names convey very little to me. Drake, I suppose, is Alfred Drake, the actor who made such a hit in *Kismet* and was the original Curly in *Oklahoma!*, but who is Nelson? Does he mean Harold Nicolson? And as for Riley, we know that his was a happy and prosperous career – we still speak of living the life of Riley – but I never heard of him as a writer. Can 'Indignant' have got mixed up and be referring to the popular hotel proprietor O'Reilly, of whom a poet once wrote:

> Are you the O'Reilly
> Who keeps the hotel?
> Are you the O'Reilly
> They speak of so well?
> If you're the O'Reilly
> They speak of so highly,
> Gawblimey, O'Reilly,
> You are looking well.

But I never heard of him writing anything, either. Evidently some mistake somewhere.

The letter continues:

I have followed the arts for some time now and can definitely state that even the works of Joshua Reynolds was not up to Shakespeare's standard.

He has stymied me again. I recall a reference to, I presume, Joshua Reynolds in a music-hall song by Miss Clarice Mayne, the refrain of which began:

> Joshua, Joshua,
> Sweeter than lemon squash you are

and gather from that that he must be an attractive sort of fellow with lots of oomph and sex appeal, whom I should enjoy meeting, but I can't place him. There is a baseball player named Reynolds who used to pitch for the New York Yankees, but his

name is Allie, so it is probably not the same man. I shall be glad
to hear more of this Joshua Reynolds, if some correspondent will
fill in the blanks for me.

Up to this point in his letter 'Indignant', it will be seen, has
confined himself to the decencies of debate and it has been a
pleasure to read him. But now, I regret to say, he descends to
personalities and what can only be called cracks. He says:

It is not my disposition to give predictions on this dispute, but let's see
how Wodehouse compares with the great bard in 2356.

Now that, 'Indignant', is simply nasty. You are just trying to
hurt my feelings. You know perfectly well that I have no means
of proving that in the year 2356 my works will be on every shelf.
I am convinced that they will, of course, if not in the stiff covers
at 12s. 6d., surely in the Penguin edition at two bob. Dash it,
I mean to say, I don't want to stick on dog and throw bouquets
at myself, but if I were not pretty good, would Matthew Arnold
have written that sonnet he wrote about me, which begins:

> Others abide our question. Thou art free.
> We ask and ask. Thou smilest and art still,
> Out-topping knowledge.

When a level-headed man of the Matthew Arnold type lets
himself go like that, it means something.

I do not wish to labour this point, but I must draw Indignant's
attention to a letter in *The Times* from Mr Verrier Elwyn, who
lives at Patangarth, Mandla District, India. Mr Elwyn speaks of
a cow which came into his bungalow one day and ate his copy
of *Carry On, Jeeves*, 'selecting it from a shelf which contained,
among other works, books by Galsworthy, Jane Austen and
T. S. Eliot'. Surely a rather striking tribute.

And how about that very significant bit of news from one of

our large public schools? The school librarian writes to the school magazine complaining that the young students will persist in pinching books from the school library, and, he says, while these lovers of all that is best in literature have got away with five John Buchans, seven Agatha Christies and twelve Edgar Wallaces, they have swiped no fewer than thirty-six P. G. Wodehouses. Figures like that tell a story. You should think before you speak, 'Indignant'.

I suppose the fundamental distinction between Shakespeare and myself is one of treatment. We get our effects differently. Take the familiar farcical situation of the man who suddenly discovers that something unpleasant is standing behind him. Here is how Shakespeare handles it. (*The Winter's Tale*, Act Three, Scene Three.)

... Farewell!
The day frowns more and more: thou art like to have
A lullaby too rough. I never saw
The heavens so dim by day. A savage clamour!
Well may I get aboard! This is the chase:
I am gone for ever.
*Exit, pursued by a bear.*

I should have adopted a somewhat different approach. Thus:

I gave the man one of my looks.
'Touch of indigestion, Jeeves?'
'No, sir.'
'Then why is your tummy rumbling?'
'Pardon me, sir, the noise to which you allude does not emanate from my interior but from that of the animal that has just joined us.'
'Animal? What animal?'
'A bear, sir. If you will turn your head, you will observe that a bear is standing in your immediate rear inspecting you in a somewhat menacing manner.'

I pivoted the loaf. The honest fellow was perfectly correct. It was a bear. And not a small bear, either. One of the large economy size. Its eye was bleak, it gnashed a tooth or two, and I could see at a g. that it was going to be difficult for me to find a formula.

'Advise me, Jeeves,' I yipped. 'What do I do for the best?'

'I fancy it might be judicious if you were to exit, sir.'

No sooner s. than d. I streaked for the horizon, closely followed across country by the dumb chum. And that, boys and girls, is how your grandfather clipped six seconds off Roger Bannister's mile.

Who can say which method is the superior?

## III

It has never been definitely established what the attitude of the criticized should be towards the critics. Many people counsel those on the receiver's end to ignore hostile criticism, but to my thinking this is pusillanimous and they will be missing a lot of fun. This was certainly the view taken by the impresario of a recent revue in New York which got a uniformly bad press. He has instructed his lawyers to file an immediate damage suit against each of his critics 'to cover the costs of their undisciplined and unwarranted remarks'. With special attention, no doubt, to the one who said, 'The only good thing about this show was that it was raining and the theatre didn't leak.' This, one feels, would come under the head of that 'slanderous volley of humourless witticisms that defies the most vivid imagination' to which the impresario alludes.

The case, when it comes to court, will no doubt be closely watched by the New Orleans boxer, Freddie Biggs, of whom, reporting his latest fight, Mr Caswell Adams of the *NY Journal-American* said that he flittered and fluttered as if he were performing in a room full of wasps. 'The only thing bad so far about the Louisiana Purchase in 1803,' added Mr Adams, 'was that we eventually got Freddie Biggs.'

I would not, perhaps, go so far as the impresario I have quoted, but I do think that an author who gets an unfavourable review should answer it promptly with a carefully composed letter, which can be either (*a*) conciliatory or (*b*) belligerent.

### *Specimen (a) The Conciliatory*

Dear Mr Worthington,
Not 'Sir'. 'Sir' is abrupt. And, of course, don't say 'Mr Worthington' if the fellow's name is John Davenport or Cyril Connolly. Use your intelligence, Junior. I am only sketching the thing out on broad lines.

Dear Mr Worthington,
I was greatly impressed by your review in the *Booksy Weekly* of my novel *Whither If Anywhere*, in which you say that my construction is lamentable, my dialogue leaden and my characters stuffed with sawdust, and advise me to give up writing and start selling catsmeat.

Oddly enough, I am, during the day, a professional purveyor of catsmeat. I write in the evenings after I have disposed of the last skewerful. I should hate to give it up, and I feel sure that now I have read your most erudite and helpful criticisms I can correct the faults you mention and gradually improve my output until it meets with your approval. (And I need scarcely say that I would rather have the approval of Eustace Worthington than that of any other man in the world, for I have long been a sincere admirer of your brilliant work.)

I wonder if you would care to have lunch with me some time and go further into the matter of my book and its many defects. Shall we say Claridge's some day next week?

Yours faithfully,
G. G. Simmons

PS. What an excellent article that was of yours in the *Licensed Victuallers Gazette* some weeks ago on 'The Disintegration of Reality in the Interest of the Syncretic Principle'. I could hardly wait to see how it all came out.

PPS. If you can make it for lunch, I will see if I can get Mrs Arthur Miller to come along. I know how much she would like to meet you.

This is good and nearly always makes friends and influences people, but I confess that I prefer the other kind, the belligerent. This is because the Wodehouses are notoriously hot-blooded. (It was a Wodehouse who in the year 1911 did seven days in Brixton Prison – rather than pay a fine – for failing to abate a smoky chimney.)

### *Specimen (b) The Belligerent*

Sir,

Not 'Dear Sir'. Weak. And not 'You potbellied louse', which is strong but a little undignified. Myself, I have sometimes used 'Listen, you piefaced child of unmarried parents', but I prefer 'Sir'.

Sir,

So you think my novel *Storm Over Upper Tooting* would disgrace a child of three with water on the brain, do you? And who, may I ask, are you to start throwing your weight about, you contemptible hack? If you were any good, you wouldn't be writing book reviews for a rag like the one you befoul with your half-witted ravings.

Your opinion, let me add, would carry greater authority with me, did I not know, having met people who (with difficulty) tolerate your society, that you still owe Moss Bros. for a pair of trousers they sold you in 1946 and that the lady who presides over the boarding-house which you infest is threatening, if you don't pay five weeks' back rent soon, to throw you out on the seat of them. May I be there to see it. That you will land on something hard and sharp and dislocate your pelvis is the sincere hope of

Yours faithfully,
Clyde Weatherbee

PS. *Where were you on the night of 15th June?*

Now that's good. That cleanses the bosom of the perilous stuff that weighs upon the heart. But don't send this sort of letter to the editor of the paper, because editors always allow the critic to shove in a reply in brackets at the end of it, thus giving him the last word.


## IV

The critics have always been particularly kind to me. As nice a bunch of square-shooters as I ever came across, is how I regard them. And one gets helpful bits of information from them every now and then. John Wain, reviewing a book of mine the other day in which one of the characters was an impecunious author living in dingy lodgings, said that this was quite out of date. Nowadays, he said, impecunious authors do not live in dingy lodgings. Where they do live, I have not ascertained – presumably in Park Lane – though as to how they pay the rent I remain vague. Still, thanks, John. A useful tip, if I ever do another impecunious author.

Of course, there are black sheep in every flock and, like all other writers, I occasionally find a brickbat mixed in with the bouquets. I was roughly handled not long ago by the man who does the book reviews on the *Daily Worker*. He called Jeeves a 'dim museum-piece' and 'a fusty reminder of what once amused the bourgeoisie'. Harsh words, these, and especially hard to bear from a paper of the large circulation and nationwide influence of the *Daily Worker*. But against this put the very complimentary remarks of the *Berlingske Tidende* of Denmark.

Its critic says (in part):

Skont Wodehouse laeses af verden over, betyder det dog ikke, at alle hat det i sig, at de er i Stand til at goutere ham. Jeg ved, at der er dannede Mennesker, som ikke vil spilde deres kostbare Tid paa hans Boger. Hvis man ikke er for Wodehouse, er man nodvendigvis imod ham, for der er kun Undskyldning for at laese ham, og det er, at man kan klukle over ham.

That is the sort of thing that warms an author's heart, but, come right down to it, I suppose the best and simplest way of getting a good notice for your book is to write it yourself. The great objection writers have always had to criticism done by outside critics is that they are too often fobbed off with a 'Quite readable' or even a '8½, 233 pp', which, they feel, do not do complete justice to their work. Getting the Do-It-Yourself spirit, the author of a novel recently published in America starts off with a Foreword in which he says:

This book is a major work of prose, powerful, moving, trenchant, full of colour, crackling with wit, wisdom and humour, not to mention a rare gift for narrative and characterization perhaps never before equalled. It is a performance which stands alone among the books of the world.

The book in question, by the way, is the story of the life of Mona Lisa and is to be published in nine volumes. The first consists of 1267 pages, and at the end of page 1276 Mona Lisa has not yet been born. But one feels that she is bound to be sooner or later, and when she is, watch for the interest to quicken.

I

And now, Winkler, we come to rather a moot point – to wit. Where do we go from here?

I know you are waiting with ill-concealed impatience for me to resume the saga of my literary career and asking yourself why I don't get on with it, but I am hesitating and fingering the chin, wondering if it would not be better for all concerned if we let it go and changed the subject. Here is the position as I see it, J.P. I have held you spellbound – or fairly spellbound – with the narrative of my early struggles, but with the publication of *Something Fresh* in the *Saturday Evening Post* those struggles ceased abruptly. Its editor, George Horace Lorimer, liked my work, and except for an occasional commission from some other magazine everything I wrote for the next twenty-five years appeared in the *SEP*. All very jolly, of course, and I would not have had it otherwise, but you do see, don't you, that it does not make a good story. Suspense and drama are both lacking.

It was at about this time, too, that I started to clean up in the theatre. Just after the appearance of my second *Post* serial, *Uneasy Money*, while I was writing my third serial, *Piccadilly Jim*, I ran into Guy Bolton and Jerome Kern. I had worked with Jerry for Seymour Hicks at the Aldwych Theatre in 1906, and the three of us now wrote a series of musical comedies, as Guy and I have related in *Bring on the Girls*, which were produced at New York's Princess Theatre and were very successful. At one time we had five shows running simultaneously on Broadway, with a dozen companies on the road.

So you see what I mean, J.P. All the zip has gone out of the thing, and I think we should take my activities from now on as read. To my mind there is nothing so soporific as an author's account of his career after he has got over the tough part and can look his bank manager in the eye without a quiver. I have known novelists, writing the story of their lives, to give not only a complete list of their novels but the plots of several of them. No good to man or beast, that sort of thing. A writer who is tempted to write a book telling the world how good he is ought to remember the reply made by Mr Glyn Johns to an interviewer at Fort Erie, Ontario, last spring.... Ah, Fort Erie, Ontario, in the springtime, with the chestnut trees a-blossom ... on the occasion of his winning the raw-egg-eating championship of Canada by getting outside twenty-four raw eggs in fourteen minutes.

A thing I never understand, when I read an item like that in the paper, is how these fellows do it. How, I mean, does a man so shape himself that he becomes able to eat twenty-four raw eggs in fourteen minutes?

One feels the same thing about performers at the circus. How did the man who dives through a hole in the roof into a small tank first get the impulse? One pictures him studying peacefully for the Church, without a thought in his mind of any other walk in life, when suddenly, as he sits poring over his theological books, a voice whispers in his ear.

'This is all very well,' says the voice, 'but what you were really intended to do was to dive through holes in the roof into tanks.

Do not stifle your individuality. Remember the parable of the talents.'

And he throws away his books and goes out to see an agent. Some sort of spiritual revelation like this no doubt happened to Mr Johns.

From his remark to the interviewer, 'I owe it all to my mother,' I piece his story together like this. His, as I see it, was a happy home, one of those typical Canadian homes where a united family lives its life of love and laughter, but he found the most extraordinary difficulty in getting any raw eggs. No stint of boiled, and on Sundays generally a couple poached on toast, but never raw. And all the time he was conscious of this strange power within him.

'If only they would let me get at the raw eggs!' he would say to himself. 'There, I am convinced, is where my genius lies.'

And one day he found his mother had forgotten to shut the door of the larder – ('I owe it all to my mother') – and saw on a lower shelf a whole dozen smiling up at him, seeming to beckon to him. It was as he wolfed the last of the twelve that he knew he had found his life's work.

'Stick to it, boy,' said that inward voice. 'Lead a clean life and practise daily, and the time will come when you will be able to manage twenty-four.'

And from that moment he never looked back.

But I was going to tell you about the reply he made to the interviewer. Asked after the final egg how he had done it, he said, 'I ate twenty-one in twelve minutes, and then I ate another three, making twenty-four in all.'

'No, I mean how did you *start*?'

'With the first egg. Call it Egg A or (1). I ate that egg, then I ate another egg, then I ate another egg, then I ate another egg, then I ate another egg, then I ate another egg, then I ate another egg and, if you follow me, so on.'

Substitute 'wrote' for 'ate' and 'book' for 'egg', and an author with a bank balance has said everything about his career that needs to be said. I, to take the first instance that comes to hand, wrote *Something Fresh*, then *Uneasy Money*, then *Piccadilly Jim*, and after that I wrote another book, then I wrote another book, then I wrote another book, then I wrote another book, and continued to do so down the years.

They are all there on my shelves – seventy-five of them, one for each year of my life – and I would love to name them all, but for the reader it would be too tedious. It is not as if I had ever written one of those historic best-sellers which everybody wants to hear about. When Noël Coward gave us the inside story of *The Vortex* and *Cavalcade*, I drank in every word, as I suppose all the readers of *Present Indicative* did, but there has never been anything dramatic and sensational about any of my productions. I have always run a quiet, conservative business, just jogging along and endeavouring to give satisfaction by maintaining quality of output. *The Inimitable Jeeves*, it is true, sold 2 million copies in America, but that was in the 25¢ paperback edition, which really does not count, and apart from that I have never stepped out of the status of a young fellow trying to get along. I would call myself a betwixt-and-between author – not on the one hand a total bust and yet not on the other a wham or a socko. Ask the first ten men you meet, 'Have you ever heard of P. G. Wodehouse?' and nine of them will answer 'No.' The tenth, being hard of hearing, will say, 'Down the passage, first door to the right.'

For the benefit of the small minority who are interested in statistics I will state briefly that since 1902 I have produced ten books for boys, one book for children, forty-three novels, if you can call them novels, 315 short stories, 411 articles and a thing called *The Swoop*. I have also been author or part author of sixteen plays and twenty-two musical comedies. It has all helped to keep me busy and out of the public houses.

There was once a millionaire who, having devoted a long life to an unceasing struggle to amass his millions, looked up from his death-bed and said plaintively, 'And now, perhaps, someone will kindly tell me what it's all been about.' I get that feeling sometimes, looking back. Couldn't I, I ask myself, have skipped one or two of those works of mine and gone off and played golf without doing English literature any irreparable harm? Take, for instance, that book *The Swoop*, which was one of the paper-covered shilling books so prevalent around 1909. I wrote the whole 25,000 words of it in five days, and the people who read it, if placed end to end, would have reached from Hyde Park Corner to about the top of Arlington Street. Was it worth the trouble?

Yes, I think so, for I had a great deal of fun writing it. I have had a great deal of fun – one-sided possibly – writing all my books. Dr Johnson once said that nobody but a blockhead ever wrote except for money. I should think it extremely improbable that anyone ever wrote anything simply for money. What makes a writer write is that he likes writing. Naturally, when he has written something, he wants to get as much for it as he can, but that is a very different thing from writing for money.

I should imagine that even the man who compiles a railway timetable is thinking much more what a lark it all is than of the cheque he is going to get when he turns in the completed script. Watch his eyes sparkle with an impish light as he puts a very small *a* against the line

4.51 arr. 6.22

knowing that the reader will not notice it and turn to the bottom of the page, where it says

(*a*) On Mondays only

but will dash off with his suitcase and his golf clubs all merry and bright, arriving at the station in good time on the afternoon of Friday. Money is the last thing such a writer has in mind.

And how about the people who write letters to the papers saying they have heard the cuckoo, Doc? Are you telling me they do it for money? You're crazy, Johnson.

## II

Although it is many years since I myself gave up writing letters to the papers, I still keep in close touch with the correspondence columns of the press, and it is a source of considerable pain to me to note today what appears to be a conspiracy of silence with regard to the cuckoo, better known possibly to some of my readers as the *Cuculus canorus*. I allude to the feathered friend which puzzled the poet Wordsworth so much. 'O Cuckoo! Shall I call thee bird or but a wandering voice?' he used to say, and I don't believe he ever did get straight about it.

In my young days the cuckoo was big stuff. Thousands hung upon its lightest word. The great thing, of course, was to be the first to hear it, for there was no surer way of getting your letter printed. The cuckoo always wintered in Africa – lucky to be able to afford it – returning to the English scene around the second week in April, and you never saw such excitement as there was from 9th April on, with all the cuckoo-hearers standing like greyhounds in the slips, one hand cupped to the right ear and the fountain-pen in the top left waistcoat pocket all ready for the letter to the editor at the first chirp.

Virtually all the men at the top of the profession – Verb Sap, Pro Bono Publico, Fiat Justitia and the like – had started their careers by hearing the first cuckoo and getting the story off to the *Daily Telegraph* while it was hot. It was the recognized *point d'appui* for the young writer.

'My boy,' I remember Fiat Justitia saying to me once after he had been kind enough to read some of my unpublished material, 'don't let editorial rejections discourage you. We have all been through it in our time. I see where you have gone wrong. These letters you have shown me are about social conditions and the political situation and things like that. You must not try to run before you can walk. Begin, like all the great masters, with the cuckoo. And be careful that it is a cuckoo. I knew a man who wrote to his daily paper saying he had heard the first reed-warbler, and the letter was suppressed because it would have given offence to certain powerful vested interests.'

I took his advice, and it was not long before editors were welcoming my contributions.

But how changed are conditions today. I quote from a letter in a recent issue of the *Observer*:

Sir,
If the hypothesis be accepted without undue dogmatism in the present rudimentary state of our knowledge that brain is merely the instrument of mind and not its source, the term soul and spirit could plausibly be regarded as redundant.

Pretty poor stuff. Not a word about hearing the cuckoo, which could have been brought in perfectly neatly in a hundred ways. I should have handled it, I think, on something like the following lines:

Sir,

If the hypothesis be accepted without undue dogmatism in the present rudimentary state of our knowledge that brain is merely the instrument of mind and not its source, good luck to it, say I, and I hope it has a fine day for it. Be that as it may, however, I should like your readers to know that as early as the morning of 1st January this year, while seeing the New Year in with some friends in Piccadilly, I distinctly heard the cuckoo. 'Hark!' I remember saying to the officer who was leading me off to Marlborough Street. 'The cuckoo!' Is this a record?

That, I fancy, is how Ruat Coelum and the others would have done it, but the letter which I have quoted is evidently the work of a beginner. Notice how he plunges at his subject like a man charging into a railway station refreshment room for a gin and tonic five minutes before his train leaves. Old hands like Verb Sap and Indignant Taxpayer would have begun:

Sir,

My attention has been drawn . . .

Before I broke into the game I used to think of the men who had their attention drawn as unworldly dreamers living in some ivory tower, busy perhaps on a monumental history of the Ming dynasty or something of that sort and never seeing the papers. But when I became a correspondent myself and joined the well-known Fleet Street club, The Twelve Jolly Letter-Writers, I found I had been mistaken. Far from being dreamers, the 'My-attention-has-been-drawn' fellows were the big men of the profession, the top-notchers.

You started at the bottom of the ladder with:

Sir,

I heard the cuckoo yesterday . . .

then after some years rose to a position where you said:

Sir,
The cuckoo is with us again, its liquid notes ringing through the
countryside. Yesterday...

and finally, when the moment had come, you had your attention
drawn.

There was, as I recollect it, no formal promotion from the
ranks, no ceremony of initiation or anything like that. One just
sensed when the time was ripe, like a barrister who takes silk.

I inadvertently caused something of a flutter in the club,
I remember, soon after I got my AD, and was hauled over the
coals by that splendid old veteran Mother of Six (Oswaldtwistle).

'Gussie,' he said to me one morning – I was writing under the
name of Disgusted Liberal in those days, 'I have a bone to pick
with you. My attention has been drawn to a letter of yours in
*The Times* in which you say that your attention has been called
to something.'

'What's wrong with called?' I said. I was young and head-
strong then.

'It is not done,' he replied coldly. 'Attentions are not called,
they are drawn. Otherwise, why would Tennyson in his well-
known poem have written:

> Tomorrow'll be the happiest day of all the glad new year,
> Of all the glad new year, mother, the maddest merriest day,
> For my attention has been drawn to a statement in
> the press that I'm to be Queen of the May, mother,
> I'm to be Queen of the May.

I never made that mistake again.

## III

Returning to Dr Johnson, I am sorry that a momentary touch of irritation caused me to tick him off so harshly. I ought to have remembered that when he said that silly thing about writing for money he was not feeling quite himself. He was all hot and cross because of the Lord Chesterfield business. You probably remember the circumstances. He had wanted Lord Chesterfield to be his patron and had been turned down like a bedspread. No wonder he was in ugly mood.

In the days when I was hammering out stories for the pulp magazines and wondering where my next buckwheat cakes and coffee were coming from I often used to think how wonderful it would be if the patron system of the eighteenth century could be revived. (I alluded to it, if you remember, in the Foreword.) No blood, sweat and tears then. All you had to do was to run over the roster of the peerage and select your patron.

You wanted somebody fairly weak in the head, but practically all members of the peerage in those days were weak in the head and, there being no income tax or super tax then, they could fling you purses of gold without feeling it. Probably some kindly friend put you on to the right man.

'Try young Sangazure,' he said. 'I know the nurse who dropped him on his head when a baby. Give him the old oil and you can't miss. Don't forget to say "My Lord" and "Your lordship" all the time.'

I have never been quite clear as to what were the actual preliminaries. I imagine that you waited till your prospect had written a poem, as was bound to happen sooner or later, and then you hung around in his ante-room till you were eventually admitted to his presence. You found him lying on the sofa reading the eighteenth-century equivalent of *Reveille*, and when he said 'Yes?' or 'Well?' or 'Who on earth let *you* in?' you explain that you had merely come to look at him.

'No, don't move, my lord,' you said. 'And don't speak for a moment, my lord. Let me just gaze at your lordship.'

You wanted, you said, to feast your eyes on the noble brow from which had proceeded that *Ode to Spring*.

The effect was instantaneous.

'Oh, I say, really?' said the young peer, softening visibly and drawing a pattern on the carpet with his left toe. 'You liked the little thing?'

'*Liked it*, my lord! It made me feel like some watcher of the skies when a new planet swims into his ken. That bit at the beginning – "Er, Spring, you perfectly priceless old thing." I'll bet you – or, rather, I should say your lordship – didn't want that one back. However did your lordship do it?'

'Oh, just thought of it, don't you know, and sloshed it down, if you see what I mean.'

'Genius! Genius! Do you work regular hours, my lord, or does your lordship wait for inspiration?'

'Oh, well, sometimes one, as it were, and sometimes the other, so to speak. Just how it happens to pan out, you know. But tell me. You seem a knowledgeable sort of bloke. Do you write yourself by any chance? I mean, write and all that sort of rot, what?'

'Why, yes, my lord, I am a writer, my lord. Not in your lordship's class, of course, but I do scribble a bit, my lord.'

'Make a good thing out of it?'

'So far no, my lord. You see, to get anywhere these days my lord, you have to have a patron, and patrons don't grow on every bush, my lord. How did that thing of your lordship's go? Ah, yes. "Oh Spring, oh Spring, oh glorious Spring, when cuckoos sing like anything." Your lordship certainly gave that section the works.'

'Goodish, you thought? I must say I didn't think it baddish myself. I say, look here, harking back to what you were saying a moment ago. How about me being your patron?'

'Your lordship's condescension overwhelms me.'

'Right ho, then, that's all fixed up. Tell my major-domo as you go out to fling you a purse of gold.'

## IV

Recently I have seemed to detect welcome signs indicating that the patron is coming back. I wrote an article the other day, in which I gave my telephone number.

'In the life of every man living in New York and subscribing to the New York telephone service' (I wrote) 'there comes a moment when he has to face a problem squarely and make a decision. Shall he – or alternatively shall he not – have his name in the book? There is no evading the issue. Either you are in the book or you are not. I am in myself. I suppose it was wanting to have something good to read in the long winter evenings that made me do it. For unquestionably it reads well.

Wodehouse, P. G. 1000 PkAv. BUtrfld 8–5029

Much better, it seems to me, than Wodak, Norma L. 404 E. 51. MUryhl 8–4376, which comes immediately before it, and Wodicka, Geo. D. 807 ColbsAv. MOnumnt 6–4933, which comes immediately after. Both are good enough in their way, but they are not

Wodehouse, P. G. 1000 PkAv. BUtrfld 8–5029

In moods of depression I often turn to the well-thumbed page, and it always puts new heart into me. 'Wodehouse, P. G.,' I say to myself. 'I000 PkAv.,' I say to myself. 'BUtrfld 8–5029,' I say to myself. 'Pretty good, pretty good.'

But – or as we fellows in the book say, BUt – there is just one objection to having your name listed – viz. that you thereby become a social outcast, scoffed at and despised by the swells who have private numbers, the inference being that you can't be very hot if you aren't important enough to keep your number a secret confined to a small circle of personal friends.

Nevertheless, I shall continue to instruct the brass hats of the system to publish my name, address and telephone number. (Wodehouse, P. G. I000 PkAv. BUtrfld 8–5029, in case you have forgotten.) A fig, if I may use the expression, for the snobs who will look down on me. What is good enough for Aaklus, Valbourg E., for the AAAAA-BEEEE Moving and Storage Company, for Zwowlow, Irving, for Zyttenfeld, Saml., and for the ZZYZZY Ztamp Zstudio Corpn is good enough for me.

Well, for weeks after the article appeared no day passed without two or three people ringing up to ask if that really was my telephone number. One of them rang up from Pasadena, California. He said – this seems almost inconceivable, but I am quoting him verbatim – that he thought my books were drivel and he wouldn't read another of them if you paid him, but he did enjoy my articles and would I like a coloured Russell Flint print of a nude sitting on the banks of the Loire. I said I would – you can't have too many nudes about the home, I always say – and it now hangs over my desk. And the point I am making is this. Whatever we may think of a man who does not appreciate my books, we must applaud what is indubitably the right spirit.

We authors live, of course, solely for our Art, but we can

always do with a little something on the side, and here, unless I am mistaken, we have the patron system coming into its own again. It should, in my opinion, be encouraged.

If any other members of my public feel like subsidizing me, what I need particularly at the moment are

> Golf balls
> Tobacco
> A Rolls-Royce
> Dog food suitable for
> > (*a*) A foxhound
> > (*b*) A Pekinese
> > (*c*) Another Pekinese
> Cat food suitable for
> > A cat (she is particularly fond of peas)
> and
> Diamond necklace suitable for
> > A wife

I could also do with a case of champagne and some warm winter woollies. And a few shares of United States Steel would not hurt.

I

Well, time marched on, Winkler, and, pursuing the policy of writing a book, then another book, then another book, then another book and so on, while simultaneously short stories and musical comedies kept fluttering out of me like bats out of a barn, I was soon doing rather well as scriveners go. Twenty-one of my books were serialized in the *Saturday Evening Post*. For the second one they raised me to $5000, for the third to $7500, for the fourth to $10,000, for the fifth to $20,000. That was when I felt safe in becoming 'P. G. Wodehouse' again.

For the last twelve I got $40,000 per. Nice going, of course, and the stuff certainly came in handy, but I have always been alive to the fact that I am not one of the really big shots. Like Jeeves, I know my place, and that place is down at the far end of the table among the scurvy knaves and scullions.

I go in for what is known in the trade as 'light writing', and those who do that – humorists they are sometimes called – are looked down upon by the intelligentsia and sneered at. When I tell you that in a recent issue of the *New Yorker* I was referred to as 'that burbling pixie', you will see how far the evil has spread.

These things take their toll. You can't go calling a man a burbling pixie without lowering his morale. He frets. He refuses to eat his cereal. He goes about with his hands in his pockets and his lower lip jutting out, kicking stones. The next thing you know, he is writing thoughtful novels analysing social conditions, and you are short another humorist. With things going the way they are, it won't be long before the species dies out. Already what was once a full-throated chorus has faded into a few scattered chirps. You can still hear from the thicket the gay note of the Beachcomber, piping as the linnets do, but at any moment Lord Beaverbrook or somebody may be calling Beachcomber a burbling pixie and taking all the heart out of him, and then what will the harvest be?

These conditions are particularly noticeable in America. If as you walk along the streets of any city there you see a furtive-looking man who slinks past you like a cat in a strange alley which is momentarily expecting to receive a half-brick in the short ribs, don't be misled into thinking it is Baby-Face Schultz, the racketeer for whom the police of thirty states are spreading a dragnet. He is probably a humorist.

I recently edited an anthology of the writings of American humorists of today, and was glad to do so, for I felt that such publications ought to be encouraged. Bring out an anthology of their writings, and you revive the poor drooping untouchables like watered flowers. The pleasant surprise of finding that somebody thinks they are also God's creatures makes them feel that it is not such a bad little world after all, and they pour their dose of strychnine back into the bottle and go out into the sunlit street through the door instead of, as they had planned, through the seventh-storey window. Being asked for contributions to the book I have mentioned was probably the only nice thing that had happened to these lepers since 1937. I am told that Frank Sullivan, to name but one, went about Saratoga singing like a lark.

Three suggestions as to why 'light writing' has almost ceased to be have been made – one by myself, one by the late Russell Maloney and one by Wolcott Gibbs of the *New Yorker*. Here is mine for what it is worth.

It is, in my opinion, the attitude of the boys with whom they mingle in their early days that discourages all but the most determined humorists. Arriving at their public school, they find themselves placed in one of two classes, both unpopular. If they merely talk amusingly, they are silly asses. ('You are a silly ass' is the formula.) If their conversation takes a mordant and satirical turn, they are 'funny swine'. ('You think you're a funny swine, don't you?') And whichever they are, they are scorned and despised and lucky not to get kicked. At least, it was so in my day. I got by somehow, possibly because I weighed twelve stone three and could box, but most of my contemporary pixies fell by the wayside and have not exercised their sense of humour since 1899 or thereabouts.

Russell Maloney's theory is that a humorist has always been a sort of comic dwarf, and it is quite true that in the middle ages the well-bred and well-to-do thought nothing so funny as a man who was considerably shorter than they were, or at least cultivated a deceptive stoop. Anyone in those days who was fifty inches tall or less was *per se* a humorist. They gave him a conical cap and a stick with little bells attached to it and told him to caper about and amuse them. And as it was not a hard life and the pickings were pretty good, he fell in with their wishes.

Today what amuses people, says Mr Maloney, is the mental dwarf or neurotic – the man unable to cross the street unescorted, cash a cheque at the bank or stay sober for several hours at a time, and the reason there are so few humorists nowadays is that it is virtually impossible to remain neurotic when you have only to smoke any one of a dozen brands of cigarette to be in glowing health both physically and mentally.

Wolcott Gibbs thinks that the shortage is due to the fact that the modern tendency is to greet the humorist, when he dares to let out a blast, with a double whammy from a baseball bat. In order to be a humorist, you must see the world out of focus, and today, when the world is really out of focus, people insist that you see it straight. Humour implies ridicule of established institutions, and they want to keep their faith in the established order intact. In the past ten years, says Gibbs, the humorist has become increasingly harried and defensive, increasingly certain that the minute he raises his foolish head the hot-eyed crew will be after him, denouncing him as a fiddler while Rome burns. Naturally after one or two experiences of this kind he learns sense and keeps quiet.

## II

Gibbs, I think, is right. Humorists have been scared out of the business by the touchiness now prevailing in every section of the community. Wherever you look, on every shoulder there is a chip, in every eye a cold glitter warning you, if you know what is good for you, not to start anything.

'Never,' said one of the columnists the other day, 'have I heard such complaining as I have heard this last year. My last month's mail has contained outraged yelps on pieces I have written concerning dogs, diets, ulcers, cats and kings. I wrote a piece laughing at the modern tendency of singers to cry, and you would have thought I had assaulted womanhood.'

A few days before the heavyweight championship between Rocky Marciano and Roland La Starza, an Australian journalist who interviewed the latter was greatly struck by his replies to questions.

'Roland,' he wrote, 'is a very intelligent young man. He has brains. Though it may be,' he added, 'that I merely think he has because I have been talking so much of late to tennis players. Tennis players are just one cut mentally above the wallaby.'

I have never met a wallaby, so cannot say from personal knowledge how abundantly – or poorly – equipped such animals are with the little grey cells, but of one thing I am sure and that is that letters poured in on the writer from Friends of The Wallaby, the International League for Promoting Fair Play for Wallabies and so on, protesting hotly against the injustice of classing them lower in the intellectual scale than tennis players. Pointing out, no doubt, that, while the average run-of-the-mill wallaby is perhaps not an Einstein, it would never dream of bounding about the place shouting 'forty love' and similar ill-balanced observations.

So there we are, and if you ask me what is to be done about it, I have no solution to suggest. It is what the French would call an impasse. In fact, it is what the French do call an impasse. Only they say amh-parrse. Silly, of course, but you know what Frenchmen are. (And now to await the flood of strongly protesting letters from Fauré, Pinay, Maurice Chevalier, Mendès-France, Oo-Là-Là and Indignant Parisienne.)

III

They say it is possible even today to be funny about porcupines and remain unscathed, but I very much doubt it. Just try it and see how quickly you find your letter-box full of communications beginning:

Sir,
With reference to your recent tasteless and uncalled-for comments on the porcupine...

A writer in one of the papers was satirical the other day about oysters, and did he get jumped on! A letter half a column long next morning from Oyster Lover, full of the bitterest invective. And the same thing probably happened to the man who jocularly rebuked a trainer of performing fleas for his rashness in putting them through their paces while wearing a beard. Don't tell me there is not some league or society for the protection of bearded flea trainers, watching over their interests and defending them from ridicule.

There is certainly one watching over the interests of bearded swimming-pool attendants and evidently lobbying very vigorously, for it has just been ruled by the California State Labour Department that 'there is nothing inherently repulsive about a Vandyke beard'. It seems that a swimming-pool attendant in Los Angeles, who cultivated fungus of this type, was recently dismissed by his employer because the employer said, 'Shave that ghastly thing off. It depresses the customers,' and the swimming-pool attendant said he would be blowed if he would shave it off, and if the customers didn't like it let them eat cake. The State Labour Department (obviously under strong pressure from the League for the Protection of Bearded Swimming-Pool Attendants) held that the employer's order 'constituted an unwarranted infringement upon the attendant's privilege as an individual in a free community to present such an appearance as he wished so long as it did not affect his duties adversely or tend to injure the employer in his business or reputation'. And then they went on to say that there is nothing inherently repulsive about a Vandyke beard.

Perfectly absurd, of course. There is. It looks frightful. A really vintage Vandyke beard, such as this swimming-pool attendant appears to have worn, seems to destroy one's view of Man as Nature's last word. If Vandyke thought he looked nice with that shrubbery on his chin, he must have been cockeyed.

And if the League for the Protection of Bearded Swimming-Pool Attendants and the Executors of the late Vandyke start writing me wounding letters, so be it. My head, though bloody, if you will pardon the expression, will continue unbowed. We light writers have learned to expect that sort of thing.

'What we need in America,' said Robert Benchley in one of his thoughtful essays, 'is fewer bridges and more fun.'

And how right he was, as always. America has the Triborough Bridge, the George Washington Bridge, the 59th Street Bridge, auction bridge, contract bridge, Senator Bridges and Bridge-hampton, Long Island, but where's the fun?

When I first came to New York, everyone was gay and lighthearted. Each morning and evening paper had its team of humorists turning out daily masterpieces in prose and verse. Magazines published funny short stories, publishers humorous books. It was the golden age, and I think it ought to be brought back. I want to see an A. P. Herbert on every street corner, an Alex Atkinson in every local. It needs only a little resolution on the part of the young writers and a touch of the old broad-mindedness among editors.

And if any young writer with a gift for being funny has got the idea that there is something undignified and anti-social about making people laugh, let him read this from the Talmud, a book which, one may remind him, was written in an age just as grim as this one.

... And Elijah said to Berokah, 'These two will also share in the world to come.' Berokah then asked them, 'What is your occupation?' They replied, 'We are merrymakers. When we see a person who is downhearted, we cheer him up.'

These two were among the very select few who would inherit the kingdom of Heaven.

I

Until this golden age sets in, if it ever does, I shall have to resign myself to the obscurity which is the fate of light writers. Not that I mind it. There are compensations to being lumped in with the other outcasts under the general head of *canaille*.

People are always coming up to me in the street and saying, 'Hullo there, Wodehouse, don't you wish you were a celebrity?' and my invariable reply is, 'No, Smith or Stokes or Bevan' (if it happens to be Mr Aneurin Bevan) 'I do not.' Nothing would induce me to be a celebrity. If in a weak moment you let yourself become a prominent figure in the public eye these days, you are nothing but an Aunt Sally for all the bright young men in the country. Debunking the eminent is now a national sport.

It was not always so. There was a time when everyone looked up to celebrities and respected them. They had never had it so good. And then suddenly everything changed. Out like a cloud of mosquitoes came a horde of young men with fountain-pens and notebooks, dogging their footsteps and recording their every unguarded speech, till today you can tell a celebrity by the nervous way he keeps looking over his shoulder and jumping if anybody whistles at him.

The only celebrity I know of who is able to cope with the

situation is Evelyn Waugh. It has probably not escaped the public's memory that a year or so ago the *Daily Express* rang him up at his Gloucestershire home and asked if their literary critic, Miss Nancy Spain, could come and interview him for a series they were running called 'A Cool Look at The Loved Ones'. Mr Waugh, who was once on the *Express* and now regards it without much favour, said No, they jolly well couldn't. Nevertheless, Miss Spain duly appeared, accompanied by Lord Noel-Buxton, who seems to have come along for the ride. Mr Waugh – Waugh the Deliverer is what most celebrities call him now – ejected them with a firm hand and having escorted them to the front gate went back to the dinner which they had interrupted.

The episode so impressed me that I reached for my harp and burst into song about it.

### THE VISITORS

My dear old dad, when I was a lad
    Planning my life's career,
Said 'Read for the bar, be a movie star
Or travel around in lands afar
    As a mining engineer,
But don't, whatever you do,' he hissed,
'Be a widely read, popular novelist.'
    And he went on to explain
That if you're an author, sure as fate,
Maybe early or maybe late,
Two jovial souls will come crashing the gate,
    Noel-Buxton and Nancy Spain.

Noel-Buxton and Nancy Spain, my lad,
    Noel-Buxton and Nancy Spain.
They're worse, he said, than a cold in the head
    Or lunch on an English train.
Some homes have beetles and some have mice,

Neither of which are very nice,
But an author's home has (he said this twice)
   Noel-Buxton and Nancy Spain.

Well, I said 'Indeed?' but I paid no heed
   To the warning words I quote,
For I hoped, if poss, to make lots of dross
And to be the choice of the old Book Soc.,
   So I wrote and wrote and wrote.
Each book I published touched the spot,
There wasn't a dud in all the lot,
   And things looked right as rain,
Till as one day at my desk I sat
The front-door knocker went rat-a-tat,
And who was it waiting on the mat?
   Noel-Buxton and Nancy Spain.

So all you young men who hope with your pen
   To climb to the top of the tree,
Just pause and think, 'ere you dip in the ink,
That you may be standing upon the brink
   Of the thing that happened to me.
That stern, stark book you are writing now
May be good for a sale of fifty thou',
   But it's wisest to refrain.
For what will it boot though it brings to you
A car and a yacht and a page in *Who's Who*,
If it also brings, as it's sure to do,
   Noel-Buxton and Nancy Spain.

Noel-Buxton and Nancy Spain, my lads,
   Noel-Buxton and Nancy Spain.
They'll walk right in with a cheerful grin
   And, when they are in, remain.
I wouldn't much care to be stung by bees
Or bitten, let's say, by a Pekinese,
But far, far better are those than these,
   Noel-Buxton and Nancy Spain.

## II

It was the *New Yorker* that started it all with its Profiles. It had
the idea that if you tracked down your celebrity, got him talking
and then went home and wrote a few thousand words showing
him up as a complete bird-brain, everybody – except the celebrity
– would get a hearty laugh out of it. They 'did' Ernest Heming-
way a year or two ago, sending a female reporter to spend the
afternoon with him and write down every word he uttered, with,
of course, the jolliest results. If you write down every word
uttered by anyone over a period of several hours, you are bound
to hook an occasional fatuous remark.

And it is not as if the celebrity got anything out of it, though
there have been indications recently that better times are coming.
The name of John Harrington is probably not familiar to my
readers, so I will explain that he is the director of sports at a
Chicago broadcasting station, and the other day he received
a stunning blow. He is still walking around in circles, muttering
to himself, and the mildest of the things he mutters is 'Bloodsuckers! Bloodsuckers!'

What happened was that he wanted to interview some members of the Kansas City Athletics baseball club and was informed
by them that they would be charmed if he would do so, provided
he unbelted $50 per member, cash in advance. No fifty fish, no
interview. It was a new experience for him, and he is living it
deeply and fully, like a character in a Russian novel.

Hats off, I say, to those Kansas City athletes. For years there
has been too much of this thing of notebooked young men sidling
up to the celebrated and getting away with all sorts of good stuff
without paying a penny for it. The celebs were supposed to be
compensated by a few kind words chucked in at the beginning.

'He looks like a debonair magician, quick and agile, in his fashionable suit of grey and elegant black patent-leather slippers.'

That was what the *Daily Express* said about Mr Cecil Beaton not long ago when he gave them an interview. A poor substitute for hard cash.

And it was an important interview, too, for in it Mr Beaton revealed for the first time the sensational facts in connection with his recent visit to the château where he has been staying in the wine country of France.

'Summer had come,' he said (Exclusive), 'and I found the atmosphere most stimulating. We had an amusing dish – a delightful creamy mixture of something I can't quite remember, but I recall truffles in it.'

All that free! The circulation of the *Express* shot up. Lord Beaverbrook was enabled to buy two more houses in Jamaica. The interviewer – and quite rightly, too, after landing such a scoop for the dear old paper – probably had her salary doubled, and was officially permitted to call Nancy Spain Nancy. But what did Mr Beaton get out of it? Not a thing except the passing gratification of seeing himself described as a debonair magician in black patent-leather slippers. Does that pay the rent? It does not. You can wear black patent-leather slippers till your eyes bubble, but the landlord still wants his so much per each week. High time those Kansas City boys put their foot down.

Though they were not the first to do it. Apparently you have to be a baseball player to stand up for your rights. I was reading the other day about an exchange of views which took place some years ago between Mr William ('Bill') Terry, at that time man-ager of the New York Giants, and a representative of the *New Yorker*, which wanted to do a Profile of him. (A *New Yorker*

Profile takes up eighty-three pages in the middle of the magazine and goes on for months and months and months.)

'And where were you born, Mr Terry?' inquired the Profile hound, starting to get down to it.

A wary look came into Wm's face.

'Young fella,' he said, 'that information will cost you a lot of money.'

That ended the love feast. They had to fill up the eighty-three pages with one of those solid, thoughtful things of Edmund Wilson's.

Hats off, therefore, also to Bill Terry. But though I approve of this resolve on the part of the celebrated to get in on the ground floor and make a bit, I am not blind to the fact that there is a danger of the whole thing becoming more than a little sordid. At first, till a regular scale of prices is set up and agreed to by both contracting parties, one foresees a good deal of distasteful wrangling.

Let us say that you are a young fellow named Grover who had bowled twenty-two wides in an over, which had never been done by a clergyman's son on a Thursday in August at Dover. It will not be long before there is a ring at the bell, followed by the appearance of a gentleman in horn-rimmed spectacles.

'Good morning, Mr Grover. I am from *Time*. Two and twenty wides in an over we understand you bowled last Thursday, and naturally anxious are all *Time* readers to hear——'

'How much?'

'£10?'

'Make it £20.'

'£15 call it, shall we?'

'Well, it depends. Are you going to refer to me as stumpy balding spectacled George Grover (28) no Laker he?'

'Certainly not. Something on the lines of a debonair magician, quick and agile, we were thinking of.'

'Yes, I like that.'

'Adding that not spoiled you has success.'

'Excellent. I don't mind knocking off ten bob for that.'

'Make it 12s. 6d.'

'No, not worth 12s. 6d. No money squanderer I.'

'Be it so. Now tell me, Mr Grover, your feelings can you describe when pouched in the gully was your twenty-second delivery?'

'I felt fine.'

'And may I say that for the sake of your wife and kiddies you did it?'

'Not for £15 you mayn't. We'd better go back to the £20 we were talking about.'

You see what I mean. Sordid. These negotiations are better left to one's agent. I have instructed mine to arrange for a flat payment of 10 guineas, to be upped, of course, if they want to know what I had for dinner at that amusing château in the wine country.

### III

The name of the *Time* man in the foregoing scene was not mentioned, but I presume he was one of those appearing in a little poem which I jotted down just now on the back of an old envelope after brooding, as I so often brood, on the list in *Time* of its editors, managing editors, assistant managing editors, deputy assistant managing editors, contributing editors, corresponding editors, sympathetic encouraging editors and what not, which is my favourite reading. You will generally find me with my feet up

on the mantelpiece, poring over this fascinating column, and it
always inspires me to bigger and better things.

> I must confess that often I'm
> A prey to melancholy
> Because I do not work on *Time*.
> It must be jolly. Golly!
> No other human bliss but pales
> Beside the feeling that you're
> One of nine hundred – is it? – males
> And females of such stature.

> How very much I would enjoy
> To call Roy Alexander 'Roy'
> And have him say 'Hullo, my boy.'

> Not to mention mixing on terms of easy
> camaraderie with

> Edward O. Cerf
> Richard Oulahan, Jr.
> Bernadine Beerheide
> Virginie Lindsley Bennett
> Rodney Campbell
> Estelle Dembeck
> Old Uncle Fuerbringer and all.

> Alas, I never learned the knack
> (And on *Time*'s staff you need it)
> Of writing English front to back
> Till swims the mind to read it.
> Tried often I've my darnedest, knows
> Goodness, but with a shock I'd
> Discover that once more my prose
> Had failed to go all cockeyed.

> So though I wield a fluent pen,
> There'll never be a moment when
> I join that happy breed of men.

And women, of course. I allude to (among others):

Dorothea L. Grine
Eldon Griffiths
Hillis Mills
Joseph Purtell
Douglass Auchincloss
Lester Bernstein
Gilbert Cant
Edwin Copps
Henry Bradford Darrach, Jr.
Barker T. Hartshorn
Roger S. Hewlett
Jonathan Norton Leonard
F. Sydnor Trapnell
Danuta Reszke-Birk
Deirdre Read Ryan
Yi Ying Sung
Content Peckham
Quinera Sarita King
Old Uncle Fuerbringer and all,
O-old Uncle Fuerbringer and all.

A pity, but too late to alter it now.

I

But though I fall short of the Luce standard and have turned out to be just one of the burbling pixies and as such more or less of a hissing and a by-word among the eggheads, I have never been sorry that I became a writer. Authorship has its ups and downs, sometimes you are on the crest of the wave, at others in the whatever it is of a wave that isn't the crest – trough, that's the word I was groping for – but taking it by and large its advantages outweigh its defects. Certainly I have done much better at writing than I would have done in some of the other professions. I am thinking at the moment of the secondhand bridge business, snail-gathering and getting hit in the stomach by meteorites.

The secondhand bridge business attracts many because at first sight it seems a quick way of making easy money. You get anything from $125,000 for a used bridge, if in reasonably good condition, and one can always do with $125,000. But – and here is the catch – it is by no means everybody who wants a used bridge. You know how it is about buying bridges, sometimes people just aren't in the mood. You might have a good year when the bridges went briskly, but there would also be those long spells when nothing seems to go right. They were trying to sell one of the New York bridges the other day, and despite all the efforts of the auctioneers to sales-talk the customers into scaring the moths out of their wallets no one would bid a nickel for it.

It was a good bridge, too. It had four trusses and between the trusses three lanes for vehicular traffic, and was capable of carrying 100,000 vehicles and 500,000 pedestrians daily. 'Give it to your girl for Christmas and watch her face light up,' said the advertisements, but nothing doing. It went begging.

The fact is, bridges are always chancy things – unreliable. You never know what they are going to do next. This is exemplified by what occurred at the re-opening of the Harrison drawbridge over the Passaic river in New Jersey the other day.

The way these drawbridges work, in case you don't know, is as follows. A boat comes along and toots, you press a button, the bridge goes up, the boat goes through, you press another button, and the bridge comes down again, and so the long day wears on. And about as attractive a way of passing a drowsy summer afternoon as one could imagine. But in 1946, having gone up to allow a tanker to pass through, this Harrison bridge stayed up and remained that way for ten years. Then the Essex and Hudson Board of Freeholders, who never stand that sort of thing indefinitely, clubbed together and raised the money to have it put back into working order, and the big day for the re-opening ceremony was fixed.

The Mayor was there. There was a silver band. Speeches were made, the 'Star-Spangled Banner' sung, and school-children paraded in droves, many of them with clean faces. Somebody handed the Mayor the scissors to cut the ribbon, and at that moment, just as he was saying, 'I hereby declare that from now on everything is going to be like mother makes it,' a tanker tooted. Up went the bridge, stayed up and is still up. If they ever get it down again, I will let you know.

There is almost no industry fuller of pitfalls than bridge-selling. I knew a man in that line who heard one day that the inhabitants of Terra del Fuego were short of bridges. It was a long way to go, and it was no joke for him having to lug his bag of samples all those thousands of miles, but he stuck it out and arrived at journey's end with the muscles of his right arm pretty stiff and sore, but with a song in his heart as he thought of the business he was going to do. The natives seemed friendly, so he decided to stay the night, and in the morning he sent in his card to a high Terra del Fuegan official.

'They tell me that you people need bridges around here,' he said.

'Not bridges,' said the official. 'Breeches.'

## II

The news in my daily paper that in certain parts of Wales the latest craze is snail-racing has turned my attention to these gasteropods after months and months during which I don't suppose I have given more than a passing thought to them.

As a writer I have always rather kept off snails, feeling that they lacked sustained dramatic interest. With a snail nothing much ever happens, and, of course, there is no sex angle. An informant on whom I can rely says they are 'sexless or at least ambivalent'. This means, broadly speaking, that there are no boy snails and no girl snails, so that if you want to write a novel with a strong snail interest, you are dished from the start. Obviously the snail-meets-snail, snail-loses-snail, snail-gets-snail formula will not help you, and this discourages writers from the outset. Almost all we know of snails from English literature is Shakespeare's brief statement that they creep unwillingly to school.

But this snail-racing should mean a change for the better and give authors more of a chance. The way it works, I understand, is that each entrant pays a small fee and the owner of the first snail to pass the judges' box takes the lot. The runners have their owners' colours painted on their shells and 'are attracted to the winning-post by a pile of wet ivy leaves', with a delirious crowd, no doubt, shouting 'Come on, Steve' or words to that effect. Any competent author ought to be able to make something of this ... the hero's fortunes depending on the big race, his snail Forked Lightning trained to the last ounce, the villain sneaking into Lightning's stable to nobble him by sprinkling him with salt, and the heroine foiling the scoundrel by removing the salt and substituting powdered sugar. There is surely a wealth of material here for something in the Nat Gould vein, and I shall probably have a go at it myself.

But when I spoke of snail-gathering as a walk in life and hinted that I did not look on it as one of the lucrative professions, I was not thinking so much of racing snails as of the ones you eat in France with garlic sauce. (If you do eat them. I wouldn't myself to please a dying grandfather.) These, I understand, flourish, if you can call it flourishing, mostly in Austria, and I was shocked to learn from a usually well-informed source that the Austrian boys who track them down are paid only sixty shillings for sixty pounds of them. (Schillings it should be really, of course, but I can't do the dialect.) Putting it more simply, they get one shilling (*schilling*) for each pound (*pcound*).

I don't know how many snails go to the pound, for it must vary a good deal according to their size and robustness. You get big beefy snails which go bullocking about all over the place – what are known in Austria as 'hearties' – and conversely you get wan wizened little snails which have stunted their growth with early cigarette smoking. Still, big or little, sixty pounds of them must take quite a bit of assembling, and I feel that what the Austrians call schnirkel-schnecke gatherers come under the head of sweated labour. But apparently Austrian fathers think differently.

'Well, Hans or Fritz or Wilhelm as the case may be,' says the Austrian father, addressing his Austrian son, 'the time has come for you to be deciding what you are going to do in the world. I myself made quite a good thing out of composing imitation Strauss waltzes, but the imitation Strauss waltz racket has gone blue on us in these rock 'n roll days, so what is it to be? The Army? The Bar? The Church? Forgery? Blackmail? Arson? Or do you see yourself making Viennese pastry?'

'Well, I'll tell you, Pop,' says the Austrian son. 'The thing I feel I have a call for is schnirkel-schnecke gathering.'

'Schnirkel-schnecke gathering, eh? Capital, Capital (*Das Kapital, das Kapital*),' says the Austrian father and pats him (we are speaking of the Austrian son) on the head and tells him to go to it and not to forget his old dad when he has cleaned up.

A misguided policy, it seems to me, because when the schnirkel-schneckes are sold to the French restaurant, the French restaurant gets about £840 11s. 5d. for the same amount of schnirkel-schneckes for which the schnirkel-schnecke gatherer, poor sap, got about £71 6s. 4d., leaving the latter down a matter of £769 5s. 1d. (check these figures).

Obviously what the boy ought to do is get a job in the French restaurant, marry the boss's daughter and become part proprietor.

## III

I don't see that there is much real money, either, in getting hit in the stomach by meteorites.

Yes, I know what you are going to say. You are going to remind me of that episode in Tennessee last year. I had not forgotten it, but I think I can show that it in no way weakens my case.

Way down in Tennessee at a place called Wading River, Mrs Jane Elizabeth Baxter, who rented a bed-sitting-room at the house of a Mrs Birdie Tuttle, was lying on the sofa one afternoon when she was surprised – and at first none too well pleased – to see a meteorite come through the roof and hit her in the stomach. Reflecting, however, that there might be money in this, she applied to a neighbouring museum and learned with considerable gratification that it was prepared to offer $2750 spot cash for this visitant from outer space.

'Pretty soft,' said Mrs Baxter to Mrs Tuttle, and was stunned when the latter claimed that since she owned the premises on which the meteorite fell, it was rightfully hers. Mrs Baxter counterclaimed that she owned the stomach on which the meteorite fell, and an action resulted. I am glad to say that it was amicably settled out of court, and Mrs Baxter paid Mrs Tuttle $50. She then sold the meteorite to the museum for $2750, and that is all she has got out of the thing. She has reached a dead end.

That is why, if I had a son and he came to me and said, 'Father, I am concluding my military service in September and shall have to be thinking of making a living. How about this meteorite business?' I should discourage him.

'Don't be an ass, my boy,' I should say. 'It'll get you nowhere.'

He then, of course, brings up the Baxter–Tuttle case. He has read about it and been greatly impressed.

'But reflect,' he says. 'Reason it out. This Mrs Baxter got $2750 from the museum, so that even after slipping $50 to Mrs Tuttle she was $2700 ahead of the game. All that from one meteorite, mark you. A meteorite a day——'

'——keeps the doctor away. True. So far I am with you, but——'

'At $2700 per meteorite per person per day, that would be $985,500 a year – or in leap year $988,200. That's nice money.'

'Ah,' I reply, 'but have you considered, my boy, that whole days might pass without a single meteorite coming your way? There must be dozens of people who don't get hit in the stomach by a meteorite more than once or twice in a good season and are simply struggling along on a pittance.'

'I never thought of that,' says the lad, and he goes off and becomes an average adjuster and does well.

And meanwhile Mrs Jane Elizabeth Baxter, in the suit of chain-mail which she now habitually wears, is lying on her sofa at Balmoral, Eisenhower Road, Wading River, looking hopefully up at the ceiling. Good luck, Mrs Baxter. I think you are living in a fool's paradise, but nevertheless good luck.

And good luck, too, to Mrs Birdie Tuttle, who is down in the cellar, listening for the crash and waiting for her cut.

I

Of course, there are many other ways of making a living open to a writer who finds himself developing into a burbling pixie and decides to go straight and lead a new life. Some are attractive, some not, and as an instance of the latter one could scarcely do better than to cite the case of Patrolman Leroy Kidwell of the town of Sedalia, Missouri.

As I had the story from a correspondent on the spot, Television Station KDRO, whose headquarters are in Sedalia, was staging a money-raising drive for the polio fund, and got from one viewer the firm offer that he would pay $5 to see Patrolman Kidwell hit in the face with a custard pie. (My informant does not say so, but, reading between the lines, one receives the impression that this viewer had something against the zealous officer.)

With Station KDRO to think is to act. It routed Patrolman Kidwell out of bed and put it up to him.

'No, sir,' said Mr Kidwell firmly. 'Not for five bucks. But I'll do it for fifty.'

Scarcely had his words been relayed to the public when calls started pouring in, and when the pledges had reached $65, the patrolman expressed himself satisfied. He appeared on the screen, took the custard pie squarely between the eyes, wiped it off and went back to bed.

Now at first sight it might seem that Patrolman Kidwell had taken the initial step leading to ease and affluence. True, on this occasion the money went to the polio fund, but next time, one assumes, Mr Kidwell would pouch the takings. He would say to himself, 'This is a good thing. I will push it along.' He was probably on the screen not more than about two minutes, and $65 for a couple of minutes' work is unquestionably good gravy. But only the vapid and irreflective would hold such an opinion long. Deeper thinkers would realize in a moment that this sort of thing, like getting hit in the stomach by meteorites, could never bring in a regular income over the years. These sudden successes are nearly always just a flash in the pan. It will probably be months before a group of citizens is again willing to pay out substantial money for the privilege of seeing custard pies thrown at Patrolman Kidwell. I shall be much surprised if a year from now he is not muttering to himself, as he walks his beat, 'Othello's occupation's gone.'

The prudent thing for anyone who wishes to provide for his old age is to find some steady job which will enable him to put by a certain something each week, so that every little bit added to what he has got makes just a little bit more, and one immediately thinks of crime, with its negligible overhead and freedom from income tax, as the solution.

Crime, especially in America, seems to be all the go these days. In New York the great thing is to stick up banks. Practically everyone you meet there is either on his way to stick up a bank or coming away from having done so. These institutions have a fascination for the criminal classes, attracting them much as catnip attracts cats. A young man went into a bank not long ago and asked to see the manager. Conducted into his office, he said he wanted a loan.

'Ah, yes,' said the manager. 'A loan, eh? Yes, yes, to be sure. And what is your occupation?'

'I stick up banks,' said the young man, producing a sawn-off shot-gun.

The manager handed over $1204 without security or argument.

Of course, you get your disappointments in this profession as in all others. Last week, a little group of enthusiasts set out to rob a bank, which involved a lot of tedious preliminary planning, not to mention the sinking of a good deal of capital in automatic pistols, tommy-guns and so on. They dashed up to the bank in their car, dashed up the steps and were about to dash through the door when they saw posted up on it the notice:

CLOSED WEDNESDAYS

And all the weary work to do over again. It was disheartening, they told one another, and they didn't care who heard them say so.


II

Nevertheless, though I fully appreciate that criminals, like all of us, have to take the rough with the smooth and cannot expect life to be roses, roses all the way, I do sometimes find myself wondering if I might not have done better on leaving the Hong Kong and Shanghai Bank to have bought a black mask and an ounce or two of trinitrotoluol and chanced my arm as a member of the underworld. When I see how well some of these under-world chaps are doing and think how little slogging brainwork their activities involve, it is hard not to feel that they are on the right lines.

Except for *Thank You, Jeeves*, which for some reason gave me no trouble at all and came gushing out like a geyser from the opening paragraph of Chapter One, I have never written a novel yet without doing 40,000 words or more and finding they were all wrong and going back and starting again, and this after filling 400 pages with notes, mostly delirious, before getting anything in the nature of a coherent scenario. A man like Charles Raynor (40) of 21 West 89th Street, New York, would raise his eyebrows at the idea of anyone expending so much energy, when all you need, if you want to put money in your purse, is to get acquainted with James Joyce in a bar and let Nature do the rest.

James Joyce – no, not the one you are thinking of – this one is a sailor who lives in Philadelphia and was recently awarded damages for losing a leg while working on his ship. When he met Charles Raynor, he had $21,000. This was speedily adjusted.

It was in a bar, as I have indicated, that Mr Joyce and Mr Raynor got together, and after a few civilities had been exchanged, Mr Joyce told Mr Raynor what a lot of money he had. On learning that what he had was only $21,000, Mr Raynor expressed surprise that he should appear so satisfied. Wouldn't he, he asked, like more? Why, yes, said Mr Joyce, he was always in the market for a bit extra, but the problem was how to get it. He could, of course, lose another leg, but for some reason he shrank from that. He couldn't tell you why, he just shrank.

Mr Raynor then said that it was a lucky day for Mr Joyce when they met. It appeared that he, Mr Raynor, had a friend, a Mr Spiller, who had invented a magic box that made $10 bills. Was Mr Joyce interested?

Yes, said Mr Joyce, he was. Interested was just the word. It was of a box of this precise nature that he had often dreamed when splicing the mainbrace and porting his helm on the seven seas. He went with Mr Rayner to Mr Spiller's residence, handed over a $10 bill, it was inserted in the box, there was a buzzing sound, and out came the $10 bill together with a second $10 bill. With a brief inquiry as to how long this had been going on, Mr Joyce parted with $6200 for working expenses, and the moment they had got it the Messrs Raynor and Spiller parted from him.

I think these two men will go far. Indeed, the police say they already have.

The methods of Betty Welsh (21) who is a gipsy were somewhat more elaborate, though she worked on similar lines. Meeting Alice Barber, a dentist's receptionist, in the street, she gave her a sharp look, asked if she might feel her pulse, and, having done so, delivered the following diagnosis: 'Yes, as I suspected, you have stomach trouble. Go home, light nineteen candles and come back to me with $30 wrapped round an egg.'

This seemed sound enough to Miss Barber. It was just the sort of thing any good New York doctor would have recommended. She followed the instructions to the letter, but it turned out that further treatment was required.

'No, not cured yet,' said Miss Welsh. 'Yours is a stubborn case. We must try again. Go home, repeat the alphabet backwards, and meet me here with a bottle of water, three potatoes and $40.'

But even this did not bring relief, and for a moment Miss Barber's medical adviser seemed nonplussed. Then she saw the way.

'Go to the jewellery store on 50th Street and First Avenue,' she said, 'get $500 worth of jewellery on credit and give it to me. That should do it.'

Unfortunately, Miss Barber told a boy-friend about it, and the boy-friend decided to take a second opinion. He called in the cops, and when Miss Barber and Miss Welsh arrived at the jeweller's, who should be waiting on the doorstep but Lieutenant Walter O'Connor and two gentlemanly patrolmen.

Interviewed later by the lieutenant, Miss Barber said, 'I had indigestion, so I thought I would give it a try.'

But while one respects practitioners like these and wishes them every success in their chosen careers, the world's worker one really admires is Robert Watson (45) of Hoboken, New Jersey, because he did down the income tax authorities – the dream of every redblooded man. He was recently convicted of having received seven illegitimate income tax refunds totalling $2500, and evidence was brought to show he was waiting for seventeen more government cheques averaging $400 each.

His method of procedure was to file a bogus return under a false name but a correct address, and then wait for the refund which he claimed. And he was just saying to himself 'Nice work, Bob. 'At's the stuff to give 'em, Watson,' when Raymond del Tufto, Jr, United States Attorney for New Jersey, came down on him like a ton of bricks, and with the usual allowance for good behaviour we shall be seeing him again in about 1961.

## III

I suppose that is really the objection to a life of crime, that the police are so infernally fussy. Over and over again they act in restraint of trade. Just before I left New York, I had a visit from the police. No, nothing I had done. I was as pure as the driven snow. What these policemen – there were two of them, a stout one and a thin one – wanted was to sell me a gadget designed to baffle the criminal classes. $8 was the price, but worth it, the stout one said, because the crime wave was becoming a regular tidal wave these days. Mounting higher every day, he said, and the thin one said 'Oftener than that' and gave it as his opinion that it was all these comic books that did it. They added fuel to its flames, he said.

The favourite trick of the criminal classes, they told me, is to come to your back door and knock on it and say they are from the grocer's, delivering groceries. When you let them in, they stick you up. The cagey thing, then, is not to let them in, and that was where you got your $8 worth out of this gadget. It is a round affair with a hole and a flap and you fix it to your back door, and when the criminal classes arrive and say they are from the grocer's, you hoik up the flap and look through the hole and say, 'Oh, you are, are you? Then where are the groceries, and why are you wearing a black mask and lugging round a whacking great gun?' Upon which, they slink off with horrid imprecations.

One can readily see where this sort of thing must lead. Back-door robberies will be stifled at the source, and those who want to turn a dishonest penny will have to do it by sticking up casual passers-by in the street, than which for a man at all inclined to shyness I can imagine nothing more embarrassing.

I know I should go all pink and flustered, if I had to do it. I can't see myself accosting a perfect stranger and saying, 'This is a stick-up.' It would sound so frightfully abrupt. I suppose the thing to do would be to lead up to it sort of.

'Oh – er – excuse me, I wonder if you could oblige me with a match? What a nuisance it is to run short of matches, is it not, when one wants to smoke. Though my doctor tells me I smoke far too much. Yours, too? Well, well, well. Dr Livingstone, I presume, ha, ha, ha. Dark here, isn't it? The evenings seem to be drawing in now, don't they? Christmas will be with us before we know where we are. Good night, sir, good night, and many thanks. Oh, by the way, there was one other thing. Might I trouble you to hand over your money and valuables?'

That would ease the strain a little, but nothing could ever make such a situation really agreeable. And suppose you happen to run across somebody deaf?

You say, 'This is a stick-up.'

He says, 'Huh?'

You say, 'A stick-up.'

He says, 'Huh?'

You say, 'A stick-up. A *stick*-up. S. for Samuel——'

He says, 'I'm afraid I couldn't tell you. I'm a stranger in these parts myself.'

Then what?

But the gravest objection to crime, to my mind, is the fatal tendency of the young criminal to get into a rut. Consider the case of the one whom for convenience sake we will call The Phantom.

I quote from my daily paper:

Lazarus Koplowitz lives at 60 Sixth Avenue, Brooklyn, where he oper-ates a candy store. Four times in the last month he has been robbed by the same man, who appears at the same time of day – 3.15 p.m. – and threatens him with the same knife. The first time, on February 3, the unwelcome caller took $10 from Mr Koplowitz. On February 10 he took another $10, as also on February 17 and February 24. Police planted a detective in the rear for some days at the calling hour, then took him away. On March 3 the marauder came back and took a further $10.

I see no future for this Phantom. He has become the slave of a habit.

I

Winkler, my dear old chap, I really must apologize. Reading
over these last chapters, I am shocked to see how I have been
rambling. You asked me a lot of questions, and instead of answer-
ing them I went wandering off on to side issues like snails and
bridges and meteorites and stick-up men and cuckoos, the last
things in the world I should imagine your newspaper and radio
public want to hear about. That is the curse with which we pixies
are afflicted. We burble. I know we had a gentlemen's agreement
that I was to survey mankind from China to Peru, but there are
limits. From now on I will buckle down to it with a minimum
of digressions, and as I see that you want information concerning
my home life, I think I can scarcely do better than begin by telling
you all about that.

As you rightly say, I am living in the country now. For seven
years I had what is called a duplex penthouse apartment on the
fourteenth floor of a building at 84th Street and Park Avenue,
New York (BUtrfld 8–5029), but now I am permanently established in the little hamlet of Remsenburg, Long Island, oddly
enough only a few miles from where I lived when I was first
married forty-three years ago. Nice house now that we have got

those two extra sun-parlours built on, and parklike grounds of about twelve acres. Why don't you come up and see me some time?

The household consists of self, wife, two Pekes, a cat and a foxhound, all of whom get along together like so many sailors on shore leave. The Pekes we brought with us, but Bill, the fox-hound, and Poona, the cat, are strays who turned up from the great outdoors and seemed to be of the opinion that this was Journey's End. They were duly added to the strength.

Their origin is wrapped in obscurity. The fact of Poona being at a loose end and deciding to clock in and take pot-luck I can understand, for Long Island is full of stray cats walking through the wet woods waving their wild tails, but Bill is a dog of mystery. He is a foxhound of impeccable breed, obviously accustomed from birth to mixing with the smart hunting set – there are several packs on the island – and why he is not getting his nose down to it with the other foxhounds is more than I can tell you. I imagine that he just got fed up one day with all that Yoicks and Tally-ho stuff, and felt that the time had come to pull out and go into business for himself.

At any rate, he appeared in our garden one afternoon and sat down, and it was plain that he considered that his future career was up to us. He was in the last stages of starvation and so covered with swollen ticks that only the keenest eye could discern that there was a dog underneath. It took a vet working day and night to pull him round with injections of liver, for practically all the blood that had been inside him was now held in escrow by the ticks. It is agreeable to be able to record that his only worry today is having to watch his calories, for he is putting on weight terribly. A fox seeing him coming now, would laugh its head off.

For human society we rely mostly on Frances, our maid, who bowls over from Westhampton each morning in her green sports-model car, the Boltons, Guy and Mrs, a few other neighbours and the local children.

One of these dropped in for a chat the other day while I was watering the lawn.

'Hi!' he said.

'Hi to you,' I responded civilly.

'Wotcher doin'?'

'Watering.'

'Oops. Have you got a father?'

I said I had not.

'Have you got a mother?'

'No.'

'Have you got a sister?'

'No.'

'Have you got a brother?'

'No.'

'Have you got any candy?'

Crisp. That is the word I was trying to think of. The American child's dialogue is crisp.

Our garden is also a sort of country club for all the dogs within a radius of some miles. They look in for a bowl of milk and a biscuit most afternoons, and there is never any shortage of birds, squirrels, tortoises and rabbits. On a good day the place looks like a zoo. And while on the subject of rabbits, I see that the New York Heart Association has found a way of making rabbits' ears droop like those of a cocker spaniel. Their doctor Lewis Thomas has discovered that the trick can be done by injecting enzyme papain into the rabbit, and the Association is pretty pleased about it all. Too easily pleased, in my opinion. I mean, let's face it. After all the smoke has cleared away, Thomas, what have you got? A rabbit from whose ears all the starch has been removed. If you like that sort of rabbit, well and good, I have nothing to say, but I think invalids and nervous people should be warned in case they meet one unexpectedly.

We know, too, where, if we should want them, we can lay our hands on a few armadillos.

One morning not long ago the telephone-answering executive of the *New York Herald-Tribune* answered the telephone, and the caller said his name was Sidney A. Schwartz. He lived at Riverhead, which is seven miles from Remsenburg, where he kept bees.

'Ah, yes, bees,' said the *Herald-Tribune* man. 'And how are they all?'

'They're fine,' said Mr Schwartz, 'but what I rang up for was to ask if you would like to have ten armadillos.'

It was a strange and interesting story that he had to relate. What gave him the idea he could not say, but one afternoon as he was looking at his bees the thought flashed into his mind – Why bees? Why not armadillos?

He knew nothing of armadillos at that time except that nobody had ever claimed that they wrote the plays of Shakespeare, but he went out and bought a couple, and it so happened that they were of opposite sexes.

Well, you know what that means in armadillo circles, J. P. Love conquers all, as you might say. And when the union of two armadillos is blessed, the result is eight armadillos, sometimes more but never less. Came a day when armadillos began to sprout in every nook and cranny of the Schwartz home, and he was soon apprised of the drawbacks to this state of affairs. In addition to requiring large quantities of dog food, frozen horse meat, cod-liver oil and cream cheese, which dented the household budget considerably, armadillos – for reasons best known to themselves

– sleep all day and come to life, like dramatic critics, only after dark. And unfortunately they are noisy and rowdy and seem to live for pleasure alone.

It was not long before *chez* Schwartz had become to all intents and purposes a night club, one of the more raffish kind, with armadillos, flushed with cream cheese, staggering about and shouting and yelling and generally starting a couple of fights before turning in for the day. It does not require much imagination to picture what it must be like with ten armadillos always around, two of them singing duets, the others forming quartettes and rendering 'Heart Of My Heart' in close harmony. Pandemonium is the word that springs to the lips.

And this is where I think that Mr Schwartz shows up in a very creditable light. Where a weaker man would have packed up and emigrated to Australia, he stayed put and rose on stepping-stones of his dead self to higher things. He had always wanted a Ph.D. degree, and here, he suddenly saw, was where he could get one. He would write a thesis on the nine-band armadillo (*Dasypus novemcinctus*) and set his name ringing down the ages. He divided the young armadillos into two groups (it was no good trying to do anything with the father and mother, they were too soppy to register) and – I quote the *Herald-Tribune*:

One group he made to walk upon a treadmill to the extent of three miles a day. The other he allowed to lead completely sedentary lives, undisturbed by anything except the thoughts that normally disturb armadillos in the springtime. And at the end of some weeks he found that the armadillos which had led the strenuous life were happier than the armadillos which had lain slothful and passive.

And he got his Ph.D., showing that out of evil cometh good, and that has cheered him up quite a lot, but I must confess that I find the reasoning of his thesis shaky. How does he know that the athletic armadillos are happier than the other lot? They may be just putting a brave face on things and keeping a stiff upper lip. You can't go by an armadillo's surface manner. Many an apparently cheery armadillo without, you would say, a care in the world is really nursing a secret sorrow, sobbing into its pillow and asking itself what is the good of it all and how can it shake off this awful depression. I should require a lot more evidence than Mr Schwartz has submitted to convince me that the ones he thinks so chirpy are really sitting on top of the world with their hats on the side of their heads.

But what interests me chiefly in the story is not the *joie de vivre* or lack of *joie de vivre* of the armadillos but the Schwartz angle. If I say that my heart bleeds for him that is not putting it all too strongly. He has got his Ph.D., yes, and that, in a way, I suppose, is a happy ending, but he has also got all those armadillos, and more probably coming along every hour on the hour. The place must be a shambles.

So if I should get the armadillo urge and wish to add a few to the dogs, cats, squirrels, rabbits and tortoises in our garden, I have no doubt that Mr Schwartz would gladly let me have them at bargain rates. I must drop over there when I can spare time and study the situation at first hand. Taking care to go in the daytime, before the cod-liver oil corks have started to pop and the night revels have begun.

One does not want unpleasantness.


II

Of sport we have no lack in Remsenburg. Over at Westhampton, five miles away, there is a good golf course and the ocean to swim in, while if one prefers not to leave the home grounds, excellent mosquito-swatting can be found down by the water at the foot of our property. Over this I, of course, hold manorial rights. The only trouble is that the mosquito season is all too brief. It ends round about the beginning of September. After that nothing remains but the flies, and a hunter who has looked his mosquito in the eye and made it wilt finds but a tepid interest in flies. One likes a tang of peril with one's sport.

Have you ever reflected, Winkler, what a miserable, coddled creature, compared with a mosquito, a fly is? It takes three weeks to breed a new generation of flies, and even then the temperature has to be seventy degrees. A spell of cold weather and the fly simply turns its face to the wall and throws in the towel. How different with the mosquito. $2 million are spent yearly in efforts to keep mosquito eggs from hatching. Lamps, sprays and drenches without number are brought into action and oil in tons poured on the breeding grounds. And what happens? Do they quail? Do they falter? Not by a jugful. They come out in clouds, slapping their chests and whistling through their noses, many of them with stingers at both ends.

Science has now established that the only mosquitoes that sting are the females. The boy-friends like to stay at home doing their crossword puzzles. One pictures the male mosquito as a good-natured, easy-going sort of character, not unlike the late G. P. Huntley, and one can imagine him protesting feebly when the little woman starts out on a business trip.

'Oh, I say, dash it! Not *again*? Are you really going out at this time of night, old girl?'

'I work better at night.'

'Where are you off to now?'

'New York.'

'You mean Newark?'

(The scene of the conversation is the Jersey marshes, where mosquitoes collect in gangs.)

'No, I don't mean Newark. I mean New York.'

'You can't possibly go all the way to New York.'

'Pooh.'

'It's all very well to say Pooh. You know as well as I do that a mosquito can only fly 200 yards.'

'I can take the Holland Tunnel.'

'Costs 50¢.'

'Oh, you think of nothing but money,' says the female mosquito petulantly, and she strops her stinger on the doorstep and goes off and probably gets squashed. Rather sad, that, Winkler. Somebody's mother, you know. Still, we cannot allow ourselves to become sentimental about mosquitoes.

As an old hunter, I like the story of the general who, captured by the Chinese in Korea, relieved the monotony of imprisonment by swatting mosquitoes. His record was a 522-mosquito day in 1953, but his best all-over year was 1952, when he bagged 25,477. The secret of success, he says, is to wait till your quarry flattens itself against the wall. The simple creature does not realize that the wall is whitewashed, and falls a ready prey to the man who, not letting a twig snap beneath his feet, sneaks up behind it with a handsomely bound copy of *The History of the Communist Party in the Soviet Union*.

They say 1958 is going to be a good mosquito year. Let us hope so, for there are few more stirring sights than a mosquito hunt with the men in their red coats and the hounds baying and all that sort of thing.

Meet you in the Jersey marshes.

## III

Compared with such centres as London, Paris or Las Vegas, I suppose one would say that life at Remsenburg was on the quite side. Or, for the matter of that, compared with Bad Axe, Michigan.

Bad Axe, Michigan, where it has been well said that there is always something doing, is the only place I ever heard of where you can get knocked down in the street by a flying cow. This was what happened the other day to Mrs Janet Whittaker of that town. She was sauntering along in a reverie, thinking of this and that, and suddenly this cow. It had been set in motion, apparently, by a passing car, and it hit Mrs Whittaker between the shoulder-blades. She was not greatly perturbed. After a sharp 'Who threw that cow?' she speedily regained her poise. When you live in Bad Axe, Michigan, nothing surprises you very much.

But though, as I say, Remsenburg lacks some of the fiercer excitements of the places I have named, it is never dull. I have my work, and there are always the hurricanes.

The two hurricanes which dropped in last year on Long Island, Rhode Island and Nantucket have proved something which I have always suspected, and that is that there is a candour and frankness about the inhabitants of the eastern states of America which they don't have out west. Ask a Californian about the San Francisco earthquake and he will hotly deny that there ever was a San Francisco earthquake. 'What you probably have in mind,' he will say, 'is the San Francisco fire.' But we easterners are open and above-board. When we get a hurricane we call it a hurricane. Stop any Long Islander or Rhode Islander or Nantucketite in the street and say, 'I hear you had a hurricane the other day,' and his reply will be, 'You betcher.' He will not

say, 'Are you alluding to last week's rather heavy fall of rain?'
Californian papers, please copy.

Talking of Nantucket, one of New York's dramatic critics was
caught there by the second hurricane. He gave it a bad notice.
It apparently split into two when it got up there, and in his review
in next day's paper he was rather severe about its lack of significant form and uncertain direction of interest. Still, he did admit
that it was intense, vital and eruptive.

Our hurricanes were Carol and Edna. Dolly, their sister, a nice
girl, went out to sea, but Carol gave us all she had got, and so
eleven days later did Edna. Though Edna, when she arrived, did
not have the same scope for self-expression. Carol had caught
us unprepared, but we were ready for Edna. Baths had been filled
with water, candles laid in. And all the trees which had not both
feet on the ground had been uprooted by Carol, so that Edna's
efforts were something of an anti-climax. Three days elapsed
after Carol's visit before the electricity came on and enabled us
to cook and have water, but with Edna we were in shape again
next day.

I am sure you will want to know, Winkler, how I got on under
conditions which would have brought a startled 'Gorblimey' to
the lips of King Lear. I rose betimes, and when the fury of the
elements had slackened off somewhat went for a refreshing dip
in the bird-bath in the garden. What a lesson this teaches us,
does it not, always to be kind to our feathered friends and never
to neglect the filling of their tubs. There was a rich deposit of
water in the bird-bath and I hopped about in it merrily. Then
back to the house to a hearty breakfast – a slice of cake and a
warm whisky and soda – and my day had begun. A sizeable tree
had fallen across the drive, rendering it impossible to get the car
out, so I walked hipperty-hipperty-hop two miles to the local

store and bought bread, milk and cold viands. Before dinner I had another splash in the bird-bath. Bed at eight-thirty.

A thing about hurricanes which I can never understand is why Cape Hatteras affects them so emotionally. Everything is fine up to there – wind at five miles an hour, practically a dead calm – but the moment a hurricane sees Cape Hatteras it shies like a startled horse and starts blowing a steady 125 m.p.h. Hysteria, of course, but why?

The great thing to do when a hurricane comes clumping along and breaking all the trees in your garden – 'Can we knock this off our income tax?' are the words you heard on every side in those days – is to look for the silver lining and try to spot the good it has wrought as well as the bad. Thus, Hurricane Edna inadvertently settled a quarrel between two neighbours of mine by removing a tree that had been leaning from one neighbour's property into the other's. The latter had commanded the former to take the damn thing out of there, and the former had refused. Harsh words and black looks. Edna settled the dispute by lofting the tree into the road, a nice mashie shot.

Carol also put 260,000 telephones out of action. This was an excellent thing. There is far too much telephoning in America. It is a pleasant thought that for three days Vera (aged sixteen) was not able to ring up Clarice (fifteen and a half) and ask her if it was true that Jane had said what Alice had said she had said about what Louise had said about Genevieve. The father of many a family of growing girls, revelling in the unaccustomed peace, must have wondered why people made such a fuss about hurricanes.

Speaking of telephones and telephoning brings to my mind a little story which may be new to some of you present here tonight. While in New York not long ago, I was one of a bunch of the boys who were whooping it up in the Malemute saloon, and the conversation turned to the subject of poise on the stage, that indefinable quality that makes the great actor or actress able to carry on unruffled when things have gone wrong and the novice is losing his or her head. One of those present instanced the case of a female star, a veteran of the American theatre, who was playing a scene with a much younger actress when the stage manager, getting his cues mixed, rang the on-stage telephone at a moment when there was no place in the play's action for a phone call.

The novice sat there petrified, but not the star. Calmly she walked to the telephone, picked up the receiver and said 'Hullo?' while her co-worker looked on reverently, feeling 'What presence! What composure!' The star stood listening for a moment, then, turning to the young actress, held out the telephone and said, 'Here. It's for you.'

But, as you were just about to remind me, J.P., this has nothing to do with hurricanes, and it was of hurricanes that we were talking, was it not? I have little more to add on that subject except to say that there is talk now of Edna and Carol's younger sister, Flossie, being on her way to Cape Hatteras, and it is a relief to see that she is described in the papers as a 'small' hurricane. They can't come too small for me. My ideal hurricane is something dainty and petite, the sort of hurricane that tries to be cute and talks baby-talk.

I

So much for the all-over picture of my home life, Winkler, but I imagine the question you are most anxious to have answered, as being of the greatest interest to your newspaper and radio public, is the one about health. Have I, you would like to know, a regimen?

I have indeed, old man. We septuagenarians must watch our health very closely if, like Old Man River, we want to keep rolling along, and the first essential, my medical adviser tells me, is to see that one does not put on too much weight. The less tonnage, the easier the heart can take it, and I am all in favour of letting my heart loaf a bit, always provided it understands that it must not stop beating.

My own weight varies a good deal from day to day, according to the weighing machine in my bathroom. The day before yesterday, for instance, it informed me – and I don't mind telling you, J.P., that it gave me something of a shock – that I weighed seventeen stone nine. I went without lunch and dined on a small biscuit and a stick of celery, and next day I was down to eleven stone one. This was most satisfactory and I was very pleased about it, but this morning I was up again to nineteen stone six, so I really don't know where I am or what the future holds.

A knowledgeable friend says the machine needs adjusting. There may be something in this.

Still, as I say, the experience has given me quite a shock, and I think it will be safest if from now on I model my dietary arrangements on those of the young Lycidas of whom the poet Milton wrote in one of his less known passages:

> ... who, weighing fifteen-three,
> Had given up potatoes, butter, beer,
> Muffins and bread and all such plumping cheer
> In timorous dread of swoll'n obesity,
> Trusting he might become
> More concave in the tum,
> Less buxom and more lithe and debonair

and strive to avoid the bad example of his friend Thyrsis in the same poem:

> Who sat him down, munching a piece of cake,
> And shook his double chin and thus bespake:
> 'This banting is a fearsome thing, God wot!'
> All rot!
> So come, thou goddess stout and holy,
> To mortals known as Roly-Poly.
> Come, too, ye sisters plump and arch
> Glucose and Stearine and Starch.
> Haste ye, nymphs, and bring with ye
> Lots of sugar for my tea,
> Lots of butter for my toast,
> Of crumpets, too, a goodly host.'
> With this he rose and puffed, as such men do.
> Tomorrow to fresh foods and dainties new.

But though I emulate Lycidas, I shall still feel that Thyrsis has the right idea. This banting is, as he says, a fearsome thing, God wot, and I think if I had my life to live over again and were given the choice I would be a corpse in a mystery story. Corpses in mystery stories always manage in some mysterious way to do themselves extraordinarily well without ever putting on an ounce.

'I have concluded my autopsy,' says the police surgeon, 'and the contents of Sir Reginald's stomach, not counting the strychnine, are as follows:

> *Caviar Frais*
> *Consommé aux Pommes d'Amour*
> *Sylphides à la crème d'Écrevisses*
> *Mignonette de Poulet Petit Duc*
> *Point d'Asperges Aneurin Bevan*
> *Suprême de Foie Gras au Champagne*
> *Neige aux Perles des Alpes*
> *Timbale de Ris de Veau Toulousiane*
> *Le Plum Pudding*
> *Friandises*
> *Diablotins*
> *Corbeille de Fruits Exotique*

and, of course, lots of sherry, hock, Bollinger *extra sec* and liqueur brandy.'

And in Chapter One Sir Reginald is described as a stern, gaunt old man with the slender limbs and lean, racehorse slimness of the Witherington-Delancys. Makes one pretty wistful and envious, that.

## II

I have always been a great reader of mystery stories or, as they now prefer to call themselves, novels of suspense, and I hold strong views on them, one of which is that the insertion into them of a love interest is a serious mistake. But the boys all seem to be doing that now. They aren't content with letting their detective detect, they will have him playing emotional scenes with the heroine.

Whoever first got the idea that anyone wants a girl messing about and getting in the way when the automatics are popping I am at a loss to imagine. Nobody appreciates more than myself the presence of girls in their proper place – in the paddock at Ascot, fine; at Lord's during the luncheon interval of the Eton and Harrow match, capital: if I went to a night club and found no girls there, I should be the first to complain: but what I do say is that you don't want them in Lascar Joe's underground den at Limehouse on a busy evening. Apart from anything else, Woman seems to me to lose her queenly dignity when she is being shoved into cupboards with a bag over her head. And if there is one thing certain, it is that sooner or later something of that sort will be happening to the heroine of a novel of suspense.

For, though beautiful, with large grey eyes and hair the colour of ripe corn, the heroine of a novel of suspense is almost never a very intelligent girl. Indeed, it would scarcely be overstating it to say that her mentality is that of a retarded child of six. She may have escaped death a dozen times. She may know perfectly well that the Blackbird Gang is after her to secure the papers. The police may have warned her on no account to stir outside her house. But when a messenger calls at half-past two in the morning with an unsigned note that says 'Come at once', she just reaches for her hat and goes. The messenger is a one-eyed Chinaman with a pockmarked face and an evil grin, so she trusts him immediately and, having accompanied him to the closed car with steel shutters over the windows, bowls off in it to the ruined cottage in the swamp. And when the detective, at great risk and inconvenience to himself, comes to rescue her, she will have nothing to do with him because she has been told by a mulatto with half a nose that it was him who murdered her brother Joe.

What we all liked so much about Sherlock Holmes was his correct attitude in this matter of girls. True, he would sometimes permit them to call at Baker Street and tell him about the odd behaviour of their uncles or stepfathers ... in a pinch he might even allow them to marry Watson ... but once the story was under way they had to retire to the background and stay there. That was the spirit.

The obvious person, of course, to rid us of these pests is the villain or heavy, and in fairness to a willing worker it cannot be denied that he does his best. And yet for one reason or another he always fails. Even when he has got the girl chained up in the cellar under the wharf with the water pouring through the grating we never in our hearts really expect the happy ending. Experience has taught us that we cannot rely on this man. He has let us down too often and forfeited our confidence.

The trouble with the heavy in a novel of suspense is that he suffers from a fatal excess of ingenuity. When he was a boy, his parents must thoughtlessly have told him he was clever, and it has absolutely spoiled him for effective work.

The ordinary man, when circumstances compel him to murder a female acquaintance, borrows a revolver and a few cartridges and does the job in some odd five minutes of the day when he is not at the office. He does not bother about art or technique or scientific methods. He just goes and does it.

But the heavy cannot understand simplicity. It never occurs to him just to point a pistol at the heroine and fire it. If you told him the thing could be done that way, he would suspect you of pulling his leg. The only method he can imagine is to tie her to a chair, erect a tripod, place the revolver on it, tie a string to the trigger, pass the string along the wall till it rests on a hook, attach another string to it, pass this over a hook, tie a brick to the end of the second string and light a candle under it. He has got the thing reasoned out. The candle will burn the second string, the brick will fall, the weight will tighten the first string, thus pulling the trigger, and there you are.

And then of course somebody comes along and blows the candle out, and all the weary work to do over again.

The average heavy's natural impulse, if called upon to kill a fly, would be to saw through the supports of the floor, tie a string across the doorway, and then send the fly an anonymous letter telling it to come at once in order to hear of something to its advantage. The idea being that it would hurry to the room, trip over the string, fall through the floor and break its neck. This, to the heavy's mind, is not merely the simplest, it is the only way of killing flies. You could talk to him till you were hoarse, but you would never convince him that better results can be obtained through the medium of a rolled-up morning paper gripped by the football coupon. I have known a heavy to sit the heroine on a keg of gunpowder and expect it to be struck by lightning. You can't run a business that way.

It is a moot point and one, I think, that can never be really decided, whether American novels of suspense are worse than English novels of suspense or, as one might say, vice versa. My own opinion is that the American variety have it by a short head. English heavies sometimes have a glimmer of sanity, but American heavies never. They are always dressing up as gorillas or something. They seem unable to express and fulfil themselves without at least a false nose. It must be very difficult to bring one of them to the electric chair.

'But *why* in order to bump off the deceased did you dress up as a gorilla?' asked counsel for the defence.

'Oh, I thought I would,' says the heavy.

'No special reason?'

'No, no special reason.'

'It just struck you as a good idea at the time?'

'That's right. It was how I saw the scene. I felt it, felt it *here*,' says the heavy slapping himself on the left side of the chest.

Counsel for the defence looks significantly at the jury, and the jury bring in a verdict of insane without leaving the box. The heavy goes to his asylum, and two months later is released as cured. Upon which, he dresses up as a Siberian wolf-hound and hurries off to rub out another citizen.

One is always seeing in the papers that some prominent person in Washington or elsewhere likes in his spare time to 'relax over a mystery story', presumably American, and I keep wondering how he manages it. The American mystery story calls for all that a man has of concentration and intelligence, if its tortuous ramifications are to be followed.

Not that you don't get some pretty testing stuff shot at you by English mystery writers from time to time. Passages, for instance, like:

'There's a reasonably good road through Slaidburn. It connects up Long Preston with Clitheroe; that is, it connects the arterial roads A65 and A59. It also connects with the railway junction at Holliford – that's the junction for your Kirkholm line. If you think it out, there's a circular route, so to speak. Kirkholm to Upper Gimmerdale by road, Gimmerdale to Slaidburn over the fells to Hawkshead and Crossdale, and Slaidburn back to Kirksdale by rail.'

'Aye, that's plain enough,' said Bord.

I am not saying that this does not tax the brain. It does, and one feels a rather awed respect for Bord, to whom it seemed plain enough. (I must get Bord to help me out with James Joyce some time.) But at least it is not pure padded cell, as are the activities of one and all in American mystery stories.

## III

But to get back to the subject of health.

In addition to watching his diet the septuagenarian must, of course, have exercise, and there I am fortunately situated. In Remsenburg we enjoy a number of amenities such as fresh air, fresh eggs and an attractive waterfront on the Great South Bay, but we have not progressed on the path of civilization so far as to have postmen. I walk two miles to the post office every day to get the afternoon mail, accompanied by Poona the cat and Bill the foxhound, who generally packs up after the first furlong or so. (Someone tells me that this is always the way with foxhounds. They have to do so much bustling about in their younger days that when of riper years their inclination is to say, 'Ah the hell with it,' and just lie around in the sun. But Poona and I are made of sterner stuff, and we trudge the two miles there and two miles back singing a gipsy song. This keeps me in rare fettle.)

Also I still do my getting-up exercises before breakfast, as I have done since 1919 without missing a day, though it is an open secret that I now find a difficulty in touching my toes, and I catch – or try to catch – Poona the cat each night. We let her out at about ten p.m. for a breath of air, and once out she hears the call of the old wild life and decides to make a night of it. This means that, unless caught and returned to store, she will hit the high spots till five in the morning, when she will come and mew at my bedroom window, murdering sleep as effectively as ever Macbeth did. And I have the job of catching her.

When you are in your middle seventies you have passed your peak as a cat-catcher. There was a time – say between 1904 and 1910 – when it would have been child's play for me to outstrip the fleetest cat, but now the joints have stiffened a trifle and I am less quick off the mark. The spirit is willing, but the flesh doesn't seem to move as it did. The thing usually ends in a bitter 'All right, be a cad and *stay* out!' from me and a quiet smile from Poona. And then the reproachful mew outside my window as the clocks are striking five. And if I leave the fly-screen open so that she can come in through the window, she jumps on my bed and bites my toes. There seems no way of beating the game.

Still, things have brightened a good deal lately owing to Poona having been bitten in the foot by another cat – no doubt in some night-club brawl – and being able to operate only on three legs. One more such episode, and the thing, as I see it, will be in the bag. I may not be the sprinter I once was, but I feel confident of being able to overtake a cat walking on two hind legs.

Meanwhile, the exercise is doing me a world of good, for apart from the running there is the falling. Owing to the activities of hurricane Carol many of the trees on the estate are shored up with wire ropes, and any Harley Street physician will tell you there is nothing better for the liver than to trip over a wire rope when going all out after a receding cat and come down like a sack of coals. It amuses the cat, too.

That is about all I can tell you, J.P., with regard to my regimen for health, except that I make a practice of smoking all day and far into the night. Smoking, as everybody knows, toughens and fortifies the system. Tolstoy said it didn't, but I shall be dealing with Tolstoy in a moment and putting him in his place.

## IV

It can scarcely have escaped the notice of thinking men, I think, that the forces of darkness opposed to those of us who like a quiet smoke are gathering momentum daily and starting to throw their weight about more than somewhat. Each morning I read in the papers a long article by another of those doctors who are the spearhead of the movement. Tobacco, they say, hardens the arteries and lowers the temperature of the body extremities, and if you reply that you like your arteries hard and are all for having the temperature of your body extremities lowered, especially in the summer months, they bring up that cat again.

The cat to which I allude is not the cat Poona which I chase at night but the one that has two drops of nicotine placed on its tongue and instantly passes beyond the veil.

'Look,' they say. 'I place two drops of nicotine on the tongue of this cat. Now watch it wilt.'

I can't see the argument. Cats, as Charles Stuart Calverley once observed, may have had their goose cooked by tobacco juice, but, as he went on to point out, we're not as tabbies are. Must we deprive ourselves of all our modest pleasures just because indulgence in them would be harmful to some cat which is probably a perfect stranger?

Take a simple instance such as occurs every Saturday afternoon on the Rugby football field. A scrum is formed, the ball is heeled out, the scrum-half gathers it, and instantaneously two fourteen-stone forwards fling themselves on his person, grinding him into the mud. Are we to abolish Twickenham and Murray-field because some sorry reasoner tells us that if the scrum-half had been a cat he would have been squashed flatter than a Dover sole? And no use trying to drive into these morons' heads that there is no recorded instance of a team lining up for the kick-off with a cat playing scrum-half. Really, one feels inclined at times to give it all up and not bother to argue.

To me, and to you, too, probably, Winkler, it is pitiful to think that that is how these men spend their lives, placing drops of nicotine on the tongues of cats day in, day out all the year round, except possibly on bank holidays. But if you tell them that, like that Phantom fellow, they have become slaves to a habit, and urge them to summon up their manhood and throw off the shackles, they just stare at you with fishy eyes and mumble that it can't be done. Of course it can be done. If they were to say to themselves, 'I will not start placing nicotine on cats' tongues till after lunch,' they would have made a beginning. After that it would be simple to knock off during the afternoon, and by degrees they would find that they could abstain altogether. The first cat of the day is the hard one to give up. Conquer the impulse for the after-breakfast cat, and the battle is half won.

But nothing will make them see this, and the result is that day by day in every way we smokers are being harder pressed. Like the troops of Midian, the enemy prowl and prowl around. First it was James the Second, then Tolstoy, then all these doctors, and now – of all people – Miss Gloria Swanson, the idol of the silent screen, who not only has become a non-smoker herself but claims to have converted a San Francisco business man, a Massachusetts dress designer, a lady explorer, a television script-writer and a Chicago dentist.

'The joys of not smoking,' she says, 'are so much greater than the joys of smoking,' omitting, however, to mention what the former are. From the fact that she states that her disciples send her flowers, I should imagine that she belongs to the school of thought which holds that abstention from tobacco heightens the sense of smell. I don't want my sense of smell heightened. When I lived in New York, I often found myself wishing that I didn't smell the place as well as I did.

But I have no quarrel with Miss Swanson. We Wodehouses do not war upon the weaker sex. As far as Miss Swanson is concerned, an indulgent 'There, there, foolish little woman' about covers my attitude. The bird I am resolved to expose before the bar of world opinion is the late Count Leo N. Tolstoy.

For one reason and another I have not read Tolstoy in the original Russian, and it is possible that a faulty translation may have misled me, but what he is recorded as saying in his *Essays, Letters and Miscellanies* is that an excellent substitute for smoking may be found in twirling the fingers, and there rises before one's mental eye the picture of some big public dinner (decorations will be worn) at the moment when the toast of the Queen is being drunk.

'The Queen!'

'The Queen, God bless her!'

And then——

'Gentlemen, you may twirl your fingers.'

It wouldn't work. There would be a sense of something missing. And I don't see that it would be much better if you adopted Tolstoy's other suggestion – viz. playing on the dudka. But then what can you expect of a man who not only grew a long white beard but said that the reason we smoke is that we want to deaden our conscience, instancing the case of a Russian murderer of Czarist times who half-way through the assassination of his employer found himself losing the old pep?

'I could not finish the job,' he is quoted as saying, 'so I went from the bedroom into the dining-room, sat down there and smoked a cigarette.'

'Only when he had stupefied himself with tobacco,' says Tolstoy, 'did he feel sufficiently fortified to return to the bedroom and complete his crime.'

Stupefied with tobacco! On a single gasper! They must have been turning out powerful stuff in Russia under the old régime.

And, of course, our own manufacturers are turning out good and powerful stuff today, so let us avail ourselves of it. Smoke up, my hearties. Never mind Tolstoy. Ignore G. Swanson. Forget the cat. Think what it would mean if for want of our support the tobacco firms had to go out of business. There would be no more of those photographs of authors smoking pipes, and if authors were not photographed smoking pipes, how would we be able to know that they were manly and in the robust tradition of English literature?

A pipe placed on the tongue of an author makes all the difference.

I

And now back to that questionnaire of yours, J.P., and let us see what else there is that you wanted to know. Ah, yes. Do I prefer living in the country to living in New York?

I do, definitely. I work better, look better and feel better. The cry goes round Remsenburg, 'Wodehouse has found his niche.'

Mark you, as a city slicker I was quite happy. I loved that duplex pnthse apt of mine. But residence in New York has disadvantages. For one thing, the telephone.

Having my name in the book, I got publicity of the right sort and my winter evening reading was all arranged for, but the trouble was that when people, curled up in the old armchair with the New York telephone directory, saw

Wodehouse, P. G. 1000 PkAv. BUtrfld 8–5029

it put ideas into their heads. Briefly, I had become, especially round Christmas-time, a sitting duck for every toucher on the island of Manhattan, and it was rarely that a morning passed without my hearing a breezy voice on the wire.

'Mr Wodehouse?'

'Speaking.'

'Is that Mr P. G. Wodehouse?'

'In person.'

'Well, well, well, well, well, well, well, well! How are you, P.G., how *are* you? Fine? Capital! No coughs, colds or rheumatic ailments? Splendid! That's wonderful. This is the Rev. Cyril Twombley. You won't know my name, but I am one of your greatest fans and simply couldn't resist the urge to call you up and tell you how much I love your books. I think I've read every line you've written. Great stuff, P.G., great stuff. Jeeves, eh? Ha ha ha ha ha.'

Well, really, I would be saying by this time, this is extremely gratifying. An artist like myself is above any petty caring for praise or blame, of course, but still it is nice to feel that one's efforts are appreciated. Furthermore, though one is too spiritual to attach much weight to that, there does sort of flit into one's mind the thought that a man as enthusiastic as this will surely buy a copy of that book of ours that is coming out next month, which will mean $52\frac{1}{2}$¢ in royalties in our kick, and may quite possibly give copies to friends. (Five friends? Ten friends? Better be on the safe side and call it five. Well, that is $2. 62 or thereabouts, and you can buy a lot of tobacco for $2. 62.)

But hark, he is proceeding.

'That was why I simply had to ring you up, P.G., old top. I just wanted to tell you what pleasure you have given me, and I am sure a great number of other people. Your sales must be enormous.'

'Oh, well . . .'

'I'm sure they are, and they deserve to be, P.G., they deserve to be. You must be a millionaire by this time, eh, ha ha ha. And that brings me to another thing I was almost forgetting to mention. Our church is getting up a Christmas bazaar and looking about for contributions and we are hoping that you will . . .'

In theory the unlisted subscriber avoids all this. If you try to get a number that is not in the book, Information tells you off good and proper.

'Sorrrrrrr-eeeeeeee, we are not allowahd to give out that numbah,' says Information, in a voice like an east wind sighing through the cracks in a broken heart.

The catch is, the unlisted boys tell me, that you keep giving it out yourself to casual acquaintances who write it down and give it to their casual acquaintances who write it down and give it to theirs, and pretty soon it is public property. I have an unlisted friend who, balancing his accounts after a certain period of time, found that his number was in the possession of twenty-three girls he no longer liked, fifty-six he had never liked, a former business associate who was suing him at the moment, a discarded masseur, three upholsterers who had made estimates for covering a sofa, and an unidentified alcoholic who rang up at regular intervals and always between the hours of three and four in the morning.

## II

Almost as grave a drawback to life in New York as the ear-biting telephonist is the New York taxi-driver or hackie.

He is quite different from his opposite number in London, partly because his name, as stated on the card on the windscreen, is always something like Rostopchin or Prschebiszewsky but principally owing to his habit of bringing with him quips and cranks and wreathed smiles like the nymphs in 'L'Allegro'. Except for an occasional gruff grunter, all New York taxi-drivers are rapid-fire comedians, and they are given unlimited scope for their Bob Hopefulness by the fact that in American cabs there is no glass shutter separating them from the customer.

There are some who place the blame for this exuberance of theirs on the newspaper men who for years have been fostering the legend of the witty taxi-driver. 'They have been exalted as a group and called brilliant conversationalists so long,' says one soured commentator, 'that they have come to believe the stories they have read about themselves and so ham it up and babble nonsense over their shoulders whenever they have a passenger who will listen.'

It may be so, but myself I think it all dates back to the time when one of them, a man who liked his joke of a morning, chanced to drive Eddie Cantor one day and on the strength of his *bons mots* got enrolled on the comedian's staff of gag-writers. The word went round that fame and fortune awaited the hackie with a good comedy routine, and the boys buckled down to it seriously, with the result that, if you take a taxi nowadays, your ride is not so much a ride as an audition. The hackie's opening words are enough to warn you of the shape of things to come.

'I want to go to the Cunard-White Star pier,' you say.

'Okay. Don't be long,' he ripostes, quick as a flash.

'You know the way there, I suppose?'

'Garsh, yes, it ain't no secret.'

Then he settles down to it. A few gay observations on the weather and he is ready for the big yoks.

'Say, mister.'

'Hullo?'

'Your name ain't Crime by any chance, is it?'

'Crime?'

'C-r-i-m-e.'

'Oh, Crime? No. Why?'

'Just thinking of a feller I had in my crate the other day. We got talking and he said his name was George Crime.'

'Odd name.'

'What I thought. Well, sir, we got to where he wants to be took and he hops out and starts walking away. "Hi, brother," I say, "ain't you forgettin' something?" "Such as?" he says. "You ain't paid for your ride." "Why would I?" he says. "Haven't you ever heard that crime doesn't pay?" Hey, hey, hey.'

You laugh politely, but inwardly you are saying, 'Not so good, Prschebiszewsky.' The build-up a little too obvious and elaborate, you feel.

He continues.

'Say, mister.'

'Hullo?'

'English, ain't you? I see by the papers there's a lot of talk over there about this hydrogen bomb.'

'So I understand.'

'Same here. Fission. That's all they talk about. Now that's a funny thing. I can remember the time when fission was a thing you did in the creek with a hook and line. Hey, hey, hey.'

If the newspaper men really are responsible for this sort of thing, they have much to answer for. The only poor consolation one has is the reflection that if this had been taking place on the stage you would by this time have been hit over the head with a rolled-up umbrella.

Only once have I been able to stem the flow. My charioteer had opened brightly and confidently, getting a few well-spotted laughs at the expense of the police force and the street-cleaning system, and then he said, 'Say, mister.'

'Hullo?'

'English, ain't you? I see by the papers there's a lot of talk over there about this hydrogen bomb.'

'So I understand.'

'Don't talk about much else, they tell me. Now that's a funny thing. I can remember——'

'Yes,' I said. 'You know how it is in England. All that interests them is huntin', shootin' and fission.'

He gave a startled gasp, and silence fell, lasting till we had arrived at my destination. My better self had woken by now and I gave him a 50¢ tip, but there was no light in his sombre eyes as he took it. The unforgivable sin had been committed. He was feeling as Danny Kaye might feel if his supporting cast started hogging the comedy. As he drove away, his head was bowed and his air that of one who has been wounded in his finest feelings.

But cheer up, Rostopchin. Tomorrow is another day, Prschebiszewsky. There will be other English clients, and I know that that sparkle will be back in your eyes as you say, 'Say, mister.'

'Hullo.'

'English, ain't you? I see by the papers ...'

And so merrily on to the pay-off.

## III

But worse than Rostopchin, worse than Prschebiszewsky, worse than the Rev. Cyril Twombley are the pigeons. One of the first things you notice if you live in New York is that there are far too many pigeons about. There are also far too many Puerto Ricans, if it comes to that, but it is the pigeons that thrust themselves on the eye and make you feel that what the place needs is a platoon of sportsmen with shotguns.

These birds are getting out of hand, and if steps are not taken a tense situation will develop. All over America there are restaurants called the Howard Johnson restaurants, owned and operated by a Mr Howard Johnson. There is one at 245 Broadway, just cross from the City Hall, and the other day the lunchers there were interested to observe a pigeon enter and start to fill up at the counter in the window where there were open bins of pecans, walnuts, pistachios and jumbo cashews. Its tastes appeared to be catholic. It would hoist up a pistachio and a couple of walnuts and lower them into its interior and then waddle along and try the pecans and the jumbo cashews, and this went on for some twenty minutes and would probably have continued indefinitely had not Mr Benjamin Meltzer, manager of the establishment's ice-cream and nut department, approached the bird from behind and enveloped it in a towel. He released it on to Broadway, and it flew away sluggishly, puffing a good deal, no doubt to get bicarbonate at the nearest drugstore.

'Tonight,' said Mr Meltzer, 'I got to clean out the window and put in new nuts, a three-hour job,' adding with some bitterness that he had worked in Howard Johnson's for six years and this was the first time he had had to wait on a pigeon. The bird, I need scarcely say, left without paying the bill.

This, as I see it, is just a beginning, the thin end of the wedge, as it were. Unless something is done and done promptly to put these birds in their place (preferably, as I say, with shotguns) the *haut monde* of New York will soon be going to the Colony or Le Pavilion for lunch and finding that pigeons have booked all the best tables.

But don't get me wrong. I am not in any sense an ailurophobe. Down in Remsenburg many of my best friends are pigeons. I keep open garden for them and you will often find half a dozen or more moaning, if not in the immemorial elms at least in the maple tree I bought last week from the nursery garden at Patchogue. What I deprecate is the drift to the towns. A pigeon in the country, fine; but in New York it just takes up space which could be utilized for other purposes. There are about a thousand of them who hang round the 85th Street entrance to Central Park, sneering at passers-by and talking offensively out of the corners of their mouths. And you have to give them bread.

I tried not giving them bread, but I couldn't keep it up. My nerve failed me. I knew they would fix me somehow. There are a hundred things a gang of pigeons can do to get back at those who have incurred their displeasure – gargling on the window sill at five in the morning, scaring the daylights out of you by tapping on the pane with their beaks, swooping at your face, pecking at your ankles . . . I couldn't risk it. Appeasement, I felt, was the only course.

The situation, then, until I moved to the country, was, briefly, this. Each year by the sweat of my brow I won a certain amount of bread, and this bread I would naturally have liked to reserve for the use of what may be grouped under the head of 'my loved ones' – myself, my wife, my two Pekinese and, of course, any guests who might happen to drop in. But much of it had to go to support a mob of pigeons who had never done an honest stroke of work in their lives.

And they weren't even grateful. Stake a pigeon to a bit of bread, and not so much as a nod of thanks. The bird just pecks at it in a disgruntled sort of way.

'Bread!' it says to the other pigeons with a short laugh, and not a nice laugh, either. 'Stale bread! He wouldn't spring a nickel for a bag of peanuts, would he? Oh, no, not Wodehouse. Know what I heard someone call him the other day? Gaspard the Miser. We'll have to fix Wodehouse.'

'Shall we commence on him now?' says a second pigeon.

'Naw, we must wait,' says the first pigeon. 'We can't do nothing till Martin gets here.'

I have no doubt that if I had not fled the city and gone into hiding in Remsenburg, I should have been rubbed out by this time.

Up in Washington, I see by my paper, they are hoping to chase the pigeons away from the Treasury Department building by stringing electric wires where they roost. The idea being that after getting a few shocks they will go elsewhere. William W. Parsons, Assistant Secretary of the Treasury for Administration, told a House Appropriation Sub-committee he thought it would work.

I can just hear the 85th Street bunch chuckling when they read about it. No, Parsons, old man, it's no good, I'm afraid. You're just a dreamer chasing rainbows, Bill, old chap. If there is one thing life has taught me, it is that there is nothing you can do about pigeons. Either you have them or you don't. It is as simple as that.

I

What next, Winkler? Television? The motion pictures? Or shall it be the changes I notice now in my daily life? Suppose I tackle those first and get them out of the way.

By the time you have reached seventy-five you do find things quite a bit different from what they were when you were in your thirties. I have been a good deal impressed these last few years, for instance, by the kindlier attitude of New York taxi-drivers towards me – their attitude, I mean, towards Wodehouse the pedestrian. Where once, after nearly running me down, they would lean out sideways and yell 'Why dontcher look where yer goin', you crazy loon?' they now merely utter an indulgent 'Watch it, grandpa.' Shows the passage of time, that, J.P. Silver threads among the gold, eh?

What other changes? Well, there is the income tax. Am I wrong, or isn't it a bit stiffer than it used to be? I seem to remember a time when, if one sold a story, one spent most of the proceeds on a slap-up dinner somewhere, but now it never seems to run to much more than a ham sandwich. I suppose income tax is necessary, but I feel it was a mistake to allow it to develop into such a popular craze.

Books, too. I find myself nowadays more and more out of tune with the modern novel. All that frank, outspoken stuff with those fearless four-letter words. It was a black day for literature, I often think, when the authorities started glazing the walls of public lavatories so that the surface would not take the mark of the pencil, for the result was that hundreds of young *littérateurs*, withheld from expressing themselves in the medium they would have preferred, began turning the stuff out in stiff-covered volumes at 12s. 6d., and more coming along all the time.

And even the purer-minded novelists are not wholly satisfactory. So many of them have such extraordinary ideas as to what constitutes age. 'He was a man not far from fifty, but still erect and able to cross the room under his own steam,' they write, or, 'Old though the Squire was, his forty-six years sat lightly upon him.' At seventy-five I have reached the stage when, picking up a novel and finding that a new character the author has introduced is sixty-eight, I say to myself, 'Ah, the young love interest.'

In real life, I must confess, I tend to become a bit impatient with these kids of sixty-eight. Noisy little brutes, rushing about all over the place yelling at one another. Want their heads smacking, if you ask me.

Another very marked change I notice in the senile Wodehouse is that I no longer have the party spirit. As a young man I used to enjoy parties, but now they have lost their zest and I prefer to stay at home with my novel of suspense. Why people continue to invite me I don't know. I am not very attractive to look at, and I contribute little or nothing to the gaiety, if that is the right word. Cornered at one of these affairs by some dazzling creature who looks brightly at me, expecting a stream of good things from my lips, I am apt to talk guardedly about the weather, with the result that before long I am left on one leg in a secluded corner of the room in the grip of that disagreeable feeling that nobody loves me. I am like the man who couldn't understand why he was shunned and thought he must have halitosis, only to discover that what kept people away from him was his unpleasant personality.

Trying to analyse my party-going self these days, I think the trouble is those paper hats. At a certain point at every American party everyone puts on paper hats and as the smiling hostess clamps mine on my brow, a sense of the underlying sadness of life sweeps over me. 'Man that is born of woman is of few days and full of trouble,' I say to myself. 'Ashes to ashes, dust to dust,' I say to myself, and, of course, this tends to prevent me being sparkling. The malaise is due, I think, principally to my spectacles. You can't wear spectacles and a paper hat and retain any illusion that you are a king among men. If hostesses would only skip the red tape and allow me to remain bareheaded I might be a social success and fascinate one and all.

And yet I don't know. Even given every advantage I think I should still remain the soggy mass of ineffectiveness which so repels my fellow-revellers and has caused so many women, parting from me, to say, 'Who was that frightful man?' The fact is, I no longer have the light touch. I am not bright. And brightness is what you want at parties. Take the case of Henry Biddle. Now there is a man whose technique strikes one as absolutely right.

Henry Biddle is a Texas oil man, and is being sued for $400,000 by a lady whom he encountered at a get-together in Bimini the other night. There was a misunderstanding, it appears, about the calypso band. Whether he wanted it to play one thing and she another, I couldn't tell you, but a sudden cloud fell on the party and it seemed to Henry that now was the time for all good men to come to the aid of it. You, Winkler, in such circumstances might have tried to help things along with an epigram or a funny story, I with one of those observations of mine on the weather, but Henry Biddle knew that this would not suffice. He hit the lady over the head with a bottle. This went well, and he hit her over the head with the bottle again. Somebody then hit him over the head with a bottle, and he stepped across to the bar, got more bottles and 'started throwing them in all directions'. The party had taken on a new lease of life.

It is possible that at this point you may be criticizing our hero's methods for a certain monotony, but you would be wronging him. The man was versatile, and this was not an end but a beginning. The hotel management, feeling that he had now livened things up sufficiently, ordered the band to intervene in the debate, and when the band advanced on him with knives, Henry ('Never at a loss') Biddle seized a fire-extinguisher and sprayed them with acid. The last seen of him before the constabulary arrived, he had backed into a corner and was swinging an electric fan around his head by its cord.

It is easy to see how this sort of thing must attract hostesses. 'Don't let me forget that charming Mr Biddle,' they say as they write their invitation lists. 'He always makes a party go so.' And they send him a special little note telling him to be sure to bring his fire-extinguisher.

Henry Biddle's tactics, of course, as he would be the first to admit, were not original. He was remembering the children's parties he used to attend as a tot where everything went, including gouging and biting. How clearly he recalled those happy, far-off binges. As if it had been yesterday he could see little Augustus beating little Gwendoline on her pink bow with a toy wheelbarrow to make her let go of the plush camel to which he had taken a fancy, while over yonder little Frank hammered the daylights out of little Alice, incensed because she had kicked him in the seat of his velvet knickerbockers.

'That's the stuff,' Henry Biddle said to himself, and reached buoyantly for his bottle.

All honour to him that after all these years he remains at heart a little child.

I

We're getting along, Winkler, we're making progress. One by one I am ticking off the questions on your list, and now to decide on which of them to settle next like the butterfly I was speaking of, the one, you remember, that flitted from flower to flower. I think I will answer your query as to whether I have ever lectured or written poetry.

No, I have never lectured. If you are an author born in England, it is a thing that is expected of you, and I have received several offers to tour the United States and make an ass of myself like the rest of the boys, but I have met them with a firm *nolle prosequi* for I know my limitations. I have only the most rudimentary gift of speech, and after reading a book I bought the other day I know that I shall never be one of those silver-tongued orators.

The book was entitled *How to Become a Convincing Talker*, and almost from the first page I saw that talking convincingly must always be beyond my scope.

'Are you audible?' it asked me. 'Are you clear? Pleasant? Flexible? Vigorous? Well modulated? Appropriate in melody and tempo? Acceptable in pronunciation? Agreeable in laughter?' And the answer was No. I was husky, hoarse, muffled, thin, indistinct, glottal, monotonous, jumbled, unacceptable in pronunciation and disagreeable in laughter, and my melody and tempo, far from being appropriate, were about as inappropriate as could be imagined.

Could this be corrected? Yes, said the book, if I followed its instructions closely. I must lie on my back with a heavy book on my chest and – first in a whisper, then loudly – repeat a hundred times the words, 'Please sell me a box of mixed biscuits, a mixed biscuit box, also some short silk socks and shimmering satin sashes,' and after that rise, stand before the mirror, stretch all my muscles, raise myself on tiptoe, throw my head back and roll it from side to side and utter the word 'Li-yah' for from five to ten minutes, finally bringing the lips back into the position of the round O.

I gave it a miss. It would have cut into my time too much. After all, one had one's life to live, one's work to do. A nice thing it would be for the reading public if, just as they were expecting another book from me, they found that I hadn't touched a type-writer for six months because I had been spending all my time standing in front of a mirror bringing my lips back into the posi-tion of the round O. I decided then and there to abandon my dream of becoming a convincing talker.

I have my moments of regret, of course. The gift of convincing talk is one that often pays dividends. Thomas Lomonaco, to take a case at random, found it a very present help in time of trouble.

Thomas Lomonaco is a taxi-driver, and he was driving his taxi not long ago at Jamaica Avenue and 75th Street, Brooklyn, when he was hailed by Elmer Hinitz.

'Gimme about 50¢ worth,' said Elmer Hinitz.

At 80th Street he produced a switch-knife and, leaning for-ward, tapped Thomas Lomonaco on the shoulder.

'This is a stick-up,' he announced.

'You don't say?' said Mr Lomonaco, intrigued.

'Yay. Slip me your money, or I will expunge you.'

'I see your point,' said Mr Lomonaco humorously, eyeing the switch-knife. Then, becoming more serious, 'Yes, the meaning of your words has not escaped me, and let me say at once that I wholeheartedly sympathize with your desire to add to your savings with times as hard as they are in this disturbed post-war era. But your dreams of picking up a bit of easy money are rendered null and void by the fact that I have on my person at the moment no cash of any description. Would it soften your disappointment if I offered you one of my cigarettes? They are mild. They satisfy.'

Mr Hinitz accepted a cigarette and the conversation proceeded along agreeable lines and as far as 118th Street, when Mr Lomonaco said, 'Say, look. Have you ever seen our local police station?'

Mr Hinitz said he had not.

'Most picturesque. Sort of pseudo-Gothic. You'll like it,' Mr Lomonaco assured him. 'What say we drive there?'

And so convincing was his talk that Mr Hinitz immediately agreed. 'A good idea,' he said, and he is now in custody, held in $1000 bail.

To reporters Mr Lomonaco stated that this was the second time he had been stuck up while pursuing his profession. The other time was in Williamsburg, where a passenger threatened him with a pistol. Mr Lomonaco, the report runs, 'talked him out of the pistol'. Obviously a man who must have spent months, if not years, lying on the floor with a book on his chest, asking an invisible shop assistant to sell him mixed biscuit boxes, short silk socks and shimmering satin sashes.

How different is the story of the two explorers who were exploring in South America and chanced to meet one morning on a narrow mountain ledge high up in the Andes where there was not space for either of them to pass. Like all explorers, they were strong, silent men, and in any case would have hesitated to speak, never having been introduced, so for perhaps an hour they stood gazing at one another in silence. Then it occurred to one of the two that by leaping outwards putting a bit of finger-spin on himself he could jump round the other. This he proceeded to do, but by the worst of luck the same thought had occurred simultaneously to the other explorer, with the result that they collided in mid-air and perished in the precipice.

This would not have happened if they had been convincing talkers.

## II

As a poet – a serious poet, that is to say – I developed late. When I was doing the 'By The Way' column on the *Globe*, I used to have to write a set of verses every morning between ten-thirty and twelve for seven years, but that was just frivolous light verse. It was only recently that I took to poetry in the true sense of the word.

They do ask the darndest questions on television in America. There is a thing on Sunday nights on one of the channels called 'Elder Wise Men', and the elderly sage they got hold of the other evening was John Hall Wheelock, the man who wrote a poem about having a black panther caged within his breast (than which I can imagine nothing more disturbing for anyone of settled habits and a liking for the quiet life).

'Tell me, Mr Wheelock,' said the interviewer, 'could you have helped being a poet?'

The implication being, one presumes, that he felt that

Mr Wheelock hadn't *tried*. He could have pulled up in time if he had had the right stuff in him, but he adopted a weak policy of drift, and the next thing he knew he was writing about panthers caged within his breast.

'I don't believe I could,' said Mr Wheelock, and the interviewer frowned censoriously and became rather cold in his manner for the remainder of the conversation.

But I doubt that the thing is always deliberate. Many who become poets are more to be pitied than censured. What happens is that they are lured on to the downward path by the fatal fascination of the limerick form. It is so terribly easy to compose the first two lines of a limerick and, that done, the subject finds it impossible to stop. (Compare the case of the tiger cub which, at first satisfied with a bowl of milk, goes in strictly for blood after tasting its initial coolie.) And the difficulty in finding a last line discourages these men from sticking to limericks, which would be fairly harmless, so they take the easier way and write serious poetry. It was after they had scribbled down on the back of the bill of fare at the Mermaid Tavern:

> There was a young lady (Egyptian)
> Who merits a word of description

that Shakespeare, Bacon, Marlowe and the Earl of Oxford realized that the rhyme scheme was too tough and they were stuck.

'Bipshion?' suggested Bacon. (He would.)

'What do you mean, Bipshion?' said Marlowe irritably. He had a hangover that morning. 'There isn't such a word.'

'Hips on?'

'Doesn't rhyme.'

'I seem to have heard people talking of having conniption fits,' said Shakespeare diffidently. 'How about "And she suffered from fits (viz. conniption)"? Just a suggestion.'

'And as rotten a one as I ever heard,' snapped Marlowe.

'Oh, dash it all,' said the Earl of Oxford. (These peers express themselves strongly.) 'Let's turn it into a play.'

And they wrote *Antony and Cleopatra*.

A similar thing happened with Tennyson's

> There was a young fellow called Artie
> Who was always the life of the party.

This subsequently became *Idylls of the King*.

## III

My own case is rather interesting. As I say, I had never written anything but light, frivolous verse, but I happened one Sunday morning to be skimming through my *New York Times* – for though well stricken in years, I can still lift my Sunday *New York Times* – and as I turned to the correspondence page of the book section I suddenly quivered in every limb. It was as though I had been slapped between the eyes with a wet fish.

The correspondence page of the book section of the Sunday *New York Times* consists of heated letters denouncing opinions expressed in letters of the previous week, and what had attracted my attention was one that began:

Sir,

I take issue with Miss U. S. Swisher...

I would like my readers to try repeating those words to themselves. I think they will find that after a few minutes their haunting beauty grips them as it gripped me. I felt that only the finest poetry could do justice to the theme, and it seemed but an instant before I was at my desk, half-way through my first serious poem.

It ran as follows:

> The day, I recall, was a Spring one,
>> Not hot and oppressive, though warm,
> The sort of a day apt to bring one
>> Right up to the top of one's form.
> So when a kind friend and well-wisher
>> Said 'Don't just sit dreaming there, kid.
> Take issue with Miss U. S. Swisher,'
>> I replied, 'Yes, I will,' and I did.
>
> It made me feel just a bit saddish
>> To crush this poor (feminine) fish:
> A voice seemed to whisper, 'How caddish!'
>> But still I resolved to take ish.
> You can't be a competent isher
>> If chivalrous qualms make you wince.
> I took issue with Miss U. S. Swisher.
>> She's never been quite the same since.
>
> So though low in the world's estimation,
>> A bit of a wash-out, in short,
> I have always this one consolation;
>> I tell myself 'Courage, old sport!
> There are others more gifted and risher
>> And plenty more beautiful, *BUT*
> You took issue with Miss U. S. Swisher,
>> So you might be much more of a mutt.'

There it might have ended and I might have given up serious poetry and gone back to light verse, but a few days later, before the afflatus had had time to wear off, I happened upon an item in my morning paper which said that researchers at Michigan State University had discovered that hens are extremely sensitive to any form of discourtesy, and I was off again.

## THE STORY OF OTIS

The tale of Otis Quackenbush is one I think you ought to hear,
So I'll relate it – and I'll try to keep it fairly short, too – here.
To make a fortune he essayed, as many people do essay,
By raising fowls in Michigan, a section of the USA.
At first the venture prospered and the eggs were large and numerous.
'Hot diggety dog!' said Otis, who was always rather humorous,
'If things go on the way they are, I'll soon, I shouldn't wonder, wear,
To keep off chills, ten-dollar bills for spring and summer underwear.'
He spoke too soon. One afternoon the hens refused to lay for him,
Which meant of course a marked decrease in what's called take-home
    pay for him.
Inside each nest he tried his best to find an egg, but was it there?
Now to, now fro he searched, but no albuminous deposit there.
He clutched his head. 'This is,' he said, 'the darnedest thing I ever
    knew.
I'd hoped for stacks of income tax to give the Internal Revenue,
But now it seems those golden dreams, so roseate and fair withal,
Have got the axe. You can't pay tax if you have not the wherewithal.'
And as, irate, he moaned his fate and started in to curse it, he
Met a friend named Hibbs, who was one of the nibs at Michigan
    University.
He told him the jam he was in. 'I am,' he said, and reticence threw
    aside,
'On the very verge of feeling an urge to end it all with suicide.'
Now Hibbs was a man who knew his hens, as one might say from
    A to Z,
And giving away this useful piece of friendly counsel gratis, said,
'The first and foremost memo every farmer has to stick in his
Notebook is this – there's nothing half so touchy as a chicken is.
Remember, then, that every hen, young, middle-aged or hoary'll
Be frightfully hurt if your manner's curt or in any way dictatorial.
And often in the summer months, when you're feeling dry and hot,
I've heard you speak quite brusquely when conversing with a
    Wyandotte.

Your clothes as well, they give an air of *laissez-faire* and messiness,
And if there's one thing hens demand, it's chic and vogue and
　　dressiness.
Those overalls you're wearing now. They're muddy. Do you roll in it?
And worse than that your old straw hat has got, I see, a hole in it.
No wonder that these hens of yours are downing tools and
　　packing up.
Your speech and deportment are in urgent need of jacking up.'
And Otis said, 'By Jove, you're right!' A new expression lit his eyes.
He had far too much sense to take offence when a friend saw fit to
　　criticize.
His upper lip grew stiff. The tip was just what he'd been hoping for.
'*Rem acu tetigisti* is,' he said, 'the phrase I'm groping for.
I see, old bean, just what you mean. The wounds that gashed my
　　breast have healed.
My ways I'll mend and be a blend of Brummel and Lord
　　Chesterfield.'
So now when Otis feeds his fowls, he wears – and very proper, too –
A morning coat, a monocle, striped trousers and a topper, too.
His mode of speech, too, once abrupt, he's disciplined until it is
Unlikely to shock a Plymouth Rock and wound its sensibilities.
He now has kegs of splendid eggs of extra special quality,
And all is gas and gaiters, not to mention joy and jollity.
If ever a farmer's heart was in a constant gentle glow, 'tis his.
It teaches us a lesson, this experience of Otis's.

After that there was no stopping me. From there to writing
'Excelsior' and 'The Boy Stood on the Burning Deck' was but
a step.

## IV

Hens, of course, are not pigs – no argument about that – but
the transition of thought between the two species is such an easy
one that I feel that this is the place to touch on the report from

Paradise, Nebraska, that the local agricultural school has discovered that if pigs are given eight dunks of whisky a day they 'acquire an optimistic view of life'. Mr John B. Fosdyke, a member of the staff of the school, says they delevelop a strong liking for these refreshers and 'get very cheerful'.

Does one or does one not shake the head? It all turns, it seems to me, on what is implied in the word 'cheerful'. Naturally, pig-lovers like their protégés to look on the bright side – a pig that goes about wrapped in a Byronic gloom can cast a shadow on the happiest farm – but one does not want them getting over-familiar with strangers and telling long stories without any point. And what of the morning after? I can see a Paradise pig being irresistibly gay and amusing all through Monday up to closing time, and on Tuesday sitting in a corner with its head in its hands and merely grunting when spoken to. There is no companion more depressing than a pig with a really bad hangover.

Paradise, in my opinion, should watch its step.

## I

You ask me, Winkler, for my views on television.

Well, I have a set, but I very seldom switch it on. I have discovered a station on the wireless where they do nothing but play music, mostly grand opera, and I prefer of a evening to read my book and listen to that. Rather the quiet, homebody type, you would call me. When some Friday night there is a big fight on, you will always find me at the ringside, encouraging Sugar Ray Robinson or Carmen Basilio or whoever it may be with word and gesture, but apart from that television scarcely enters my life.

I know enough about the industry, of course, to be able to understand the technical terms connected with it.

For example:

*Intimate Show* A comedy programme with no laughs.

*Situation Comedy* A programme that has the same story every week.

*Satire* Jokes which do not get laughs.

*Fresh Humour* Old sure-fire jokes told by a young comedian.

*Literate Humour* Old sure-fire jokes told by a young comedian with horn-rimmed spectacles.

*Song Stylist* A singer.

*Internationally Famous Song Stylist* A singer.

*Singing Personality* A lousy singer.
*Long-term Contract* A contract.
*Seven-year Contract* A contract for six weeks.
*$10,000 a week salary* $500.

But beyond this you might say that television is a sealed book to me and one which I doubt if I shall ever open again except on Friday nights.

I am told by friends who follow all the programmes that by abstaining in this manner I miss a lot of good things. The other night, for instance, there appeared on the screen, demonstrating a mattress, a well-upholstered young woman who was introduced as Miss Foam Bedding of 1957 and was well worth more than a passing glance. (It is virtually impossible in America nowadays for a girl not to be Miss Something. A friend of a friend of mine is acquainted with a lady who has the job of putting imitation orange pips into tinned orange juice in order to create the illusion that the beverage has been freshly squeezed from the parent fruit. She is expecting any day to become Miss Ersatz Orange Pip of 1957.)

And then there was the man who was doing a cigarette commercial and fell into one of those sudden fits of dreaminess and abstraction which all of us experience now and then. He went through all the motions perfectly correctly. He drew in a mouthful of smoke, blew it out slowly, watching it curl over his head and smiled a smile of just the right degree of revoltingness. Where he went wrong was in saying, 'Man, man! This is *real* coffee!' Might have happened to any of us, of course, but I think he was wise to enrol himself next day in the Dr Bruno Furst School of Memory and Concentration.

I sometimes think, looking back to the time when I was a

viewer, that I could have endured television with more fortitude if they had not laughed so much all the time. Turning on the set after reading the morning paper was like coming out of the shadows into a world of sunshine.

American papers today go in exclusively for gloom. I never saw so many people viewing with concern and contemplating with the gravest apprehension as are writing now for the daily press of the country. Talk about looking on the dark side. The only ones who do not prophesy the collapse of civilization at 3.30 sharp (Eastern Standard Time) a week from Wednesday are those who make it Tuesday afternoon at 2.45. But twiddle that knob and everything is gaiety and happiness and the laughter of little children.

At least, one assumes that they are little children. On the evidence submitted I would say their mental age was about six. Everybody is laughing on television these days. The studio audiences have, of course, been laughing themselves sick for years on the most flimsy provocation, but now the contagion has spread to the performers.

The other day John Crosby – not to be confused with Bing: Bing sings – John is the fellow who watches television for the New York *Herald-Tribune*, than which I can imagine no more appalling job – just think of *having* to watch television – you don't catch John Crosby singing – he groans a good deal, so that you may think he is singing, but . . . Where was I? I seem to have lost the thread. Ah, yes, John Crosby. My reason for bringing him up was that he was complaining the other day about the time when Senator Margaret Chase Smith interviewed the Burmese Premier U Nu on television and U Nu was so doubled up with laughter throughout that you could scarcely follow what he was saying. It came out something like this:

'If aggression – ha, ha, ha – comes from a foe – ha, ha, ha – the United Nations are quite ready to pass resolutions condemning that foe, but – wait, folks, you ain't heard nothin' yet – when aggression comes from friends, they like – this is going to have you in stitches – they like to keep a little quiet – ha, ha, ha – or even if they are not quiet, they don't do full justice – ho, ho, ho.'

The whole punctuated with roars of merriment from the studio audience. No wonder John Crosby screams thinly and jumps six feet up in the air if you tap him unexpectedly on the shoulder. Just a bundle of nerves, our John.

The gruesome thing is that this is not always the laughter of a real studio audience. Frequently, it is tinned or bottled. They preserve it on sound tracks, often dating back for years, so that what you are getting is the mummified mirth of people who, in many cases, died way back in about 1946, and if that is not an eerie thought, what is? 'The voice I hear this passing night was heard in ancient days by emperor and clown,' as Keats put it, switching off the comedy programme.

Furthermore, somebody has invented what is known as a laugh machine which can produce completely artificial laughter. The man in charge of it keeps pressing a button at intervals during the cross-talk act, and the comedians love it.

Living-laughter studio audiences, as opposed to laugh machines and those indomitable wraiths who, in spite of having passed beyond the veil, are still in the highest spirits and always ready to do their bit, seem to be governed by some code of rules, probably unwritten and conveyed by word of mouth, for it is surely straining the probabilities a good deal to assume that a studio audience can read. It is a code subject to alteration without notice, and a certain amount of confusion sometimes results. Thus, in the United States it used to be obligatory to laugh whenever anyone on the television screen mentioned Brooklyn. If there was one credo rooted in the minds of the citizenry it was that the word Brooklyn was cachinnogenic. And now there has been a change of policy, and today you have to laugh at Texas.

Nobody knows why. It is just an order that has come down from the men higher up. It is perfectly permissible under the new rules to keep a straight face when somebody speaks of Flatbush or the Gowanus Canal, but a studio audience which fails to laugh at the story of the Texan who refused steak *aux champignons* because he did not like champagne poured over his steak soon finds itself purged. The secret police are knocking at its door before it knows where it is.

But there is a fine spirit stirring in America these days, I am glad to say. The people are on the march. The other day someone whipped out a revolver and shot his television set, and a week or so ago there was a still more impressive demonstration. Folks, let me lead by the hand into the Hall of Fame, Richard Wilton.

At one-thirty in the afternoon of what will no doubt be known as Wilton's Day and celebrated as a national festival, Richard Wilton (29), of 103 Baker Avenue, Brooklyn, entered the studio of the Columbia Broadcasting Company during the rehearsal of a television show, armed with an eight-inch carving knife.

'I hate all television!' he announced. 'I hate commentators. I hate the whole lousy bunch. There ought to be a law against television. I want to kill a TV operator.'

Having spoken these words, which must have touched a responsive chord in many a bosom, this splendid fellow proceeded to stab a cameraman and to hit the producer on the frontal bone with a carafe. And lest you purse your lips at the latter statement, saying to yourselves, 'Hullo! What's this? Did Wilton weaken?' I must explain that a carafe, picked up on the set, was all he had to work with. After he stabbed the camera-man, the knife broke. He had paid only 59¢ for it, not reflecting that you cannot get a really good carving knife as cheap as that. If you are going to stab cameramen, it is always wisest to go as high as a dollar.

It was as he was about to attack the director that the police came in and scooped him up, a sad disappointment to the better element. It appears that there is some law against wiping out television directors with carafes, one of those strange laws that get passed occasionally, nobody knows why.

Where Richard went wrong, in my opinion, was in confining his activities to a rehearsal, for by doing so he missed the studio audience. He should have bided his time till one of these gangs had been assembled.

Where everything about television is so frightful, it is difficult to say which is its most repulsive feature, but the majority of connoisseurs would, I think, pick the studio audience. If it would only stay quiet, nobody would have any complaint, but it won't. It laughs like a congregation of hyenas at everything. The other night on what was for some reason described as a comedy pro-gramme a girl said to a man, 'You are selfish.'

To which he replied, 'How dare you call me a shellfish?'

The studio audience let out a bellow of mirth which was audible as far downtown as the Battery, and all over America strong men gritted their teeth and muttered, 'Wilton, thou shouldst be living at this hour!'

But a time will come. In ninety days or whatever it is he will be with us once more. Good hunting, Richard Wilton. And don't make that mistake again of trying to do it on the cheap. Avoid bargain prices. Even if it costs as much as $2, get a good knife.

## II

From the foregoing remarks you may have formed the impression that I dislike television. I would not go as far as to say that. Apart from thinking it the foulest, ghastliest, loathsomest nightmare ever inflicted by science on a suffering human race, and the programmes, except for those Friday-night fights, the most drivelling half-witted productions ever seen outside Guest Night at a home for the feeble-minded, I do not particularly object to it. As far as I am concerned, it can carry on, provided – I say provided – I have not to excite the derision of the mob by appearing on the screen myself.

But how often this happens. Every time I have a new book out, it comes again ... the Finger. The telephone rings, and it is my publishers' publicity man informing me briskly that I am to appear on television next week – Monday 8.30, Sonny Booch's 'Strictly for Morons' half-hour; Tuesday, 9.15, Alonzo Todd's 'Park Your Brains in the Cloakroom'; and Thursday, 7.35, Genevieve Goole Pobsleigh's 'Life Among the Halfwits'.

You might suppose from all this that there is a great popular demand for me, that America wants Wodehouse and refuses to be put off with President Eisenhower and similar cheap substitutes, but this is not so. The explanation is that this publicity man thinks it will boost the sales of my book if I am seen by millions on the television screen, not realizing that the one way of slaying a book is to let the people get a look at the author.

Authors as a class are no oil-paintings. You have only to go to one of those literary dinners to test the truth of this. At such a binge you will see tall authors, short authors, stout authors, thin authors and authors of medium height and girth, but all of these authors without exception look like something that would be passed over with a disdainful jerk of the beak by the least fastidious buzzard in the Gobi desert. Only very rarely do we find one who has even the most rudimentary resemblance to anything part-human.

If they wanted to interview me on the radio, that would be different. I have an attractive voice, rich, mellow, with certain deep organ tones in it calculated to make quite a number of the cash customers dig up the $3.50. But it is fatal to let them see me.

Owing to my having become mentally arrested at an early age, I write the sort of books which people, not knowing the facts, assume to be the work of a cheerful, if backward, young fellow of about twenty-five. 'Well, well,' they tell one another, 'we might do worse than hear what this youngster has to say. Get the rising generation point of view, and all that.' And what happens? 'We have with us tonight Mr P. G. Wodehouse' ... and on totters a spavined septuagenarian, his bald head coated with pancake flour to keep it from shining and his palsied limbs twitching feebly like those of a galvanized frog. Little wonder that when the half-yearly score sheet reaches me some months later I find that sales have been what publishers call 'slow' again. America's book-buyers have decided as one book-buyer to keep the money in the old oak chest, and I don't blame them. I wouldn't risk twopence on anyone who looks as I do on the television screen.

I have never understood this theory that you don't get the full flavour of a writer's work unless you see him. On every newspaper staff in America there are half a dozen columnists, and every day each of these columnists has his photograph at the head of his column. All wrong it seems to me. I mean, after you have seen these gifted – but not frightfully ornamental – men 300 or 400 days in succession you have had practically all you require and their spell wanes. It is a significant thing, I think, that the greatest of all columnists, Walter Winchell, who has led the field for a matter of twenty-five years, has never allowed his photograph to appear. And Walter is a good-looking man, too, not unlike what I was in my prime.

That is the maddening thing about this television business, that they are catching me too late. 'Oh, God, put back Thy universe and give me yesterday,' as the fellow said. Well, no, not yesterday perhaps, but say 1906 or thereabouts. I really was an eyeful then. Trim athletic figure, finely chiselled features and more hair on the top of my head than you could shake a stick at. I would have been perfectly willing to exhibit myself to America's millions then. But now I have definitely gone off quite a bit, and that is why, when this publicity man rings up, I have my answer ready, quick as a flash.

'Terribly sorry,' I say. 'I'm just off to the Coast.'

Heaven bless the Coast. It is the one safe refuge. Even press representatives or public relations lizards or whatever they call themselves know they can't get at you there. And these constant visits to the Coast are improving my prestige. 'Wodehouse always seems to be going to Hollywood,' people say. 'Yes,' reply the people these people are addressing, 'the demand for him in the studios is tremendous.' 'Odd one never sees his name on screen credits,' says the first people. 'Oh no,' (second people speaking). 'He writes under a number of pseudonyms. Makes a fortune, I understand.'

I

As a matter of fact, I have been to Hollywood, though not recently. I went there in 1930. I had a year's contract, and was required to do so little work in return for the money I received that I was able in the twelve months before I became a fugitive from the chain-gang to write a novel and nine short stories, besides brushing up my golf, getting an attractive sun-tan and perfecting my Australian crawl in the swimming-pool.

It is all sadly changed now, they tell me. Once a combination of Santa Claus and Good-Time Charlie, Hollywood has become a Scrooge. The dear old days are dead and the spirit of cheerful giving a thing of the past. But in 1930 the talkies had just started, and the slogan was Come one, come all, and the more the merrier. It was an era when only a man of exceptional ability and determination could keep from getting signed up by a studio in some capacity or other. I happened to be engaged as a writer, but I might quite as easily have been scooped in as a technical adviser or a vocal instructor. (At least I had a roof to my mouth, which many vocal instructors in Hollywood at that time had not.) The heartiness and hospitality reminded one of the Jolly Innkeeper (with entrance number in Act One) of the old-style comic opera.

One can understand it, of course. The advent of sound had

made the manufacture of motion pictures an infinitely more complex affair than it had been up till then. In the silent days everything had been informal and casual, just a lot of great big happy schoolboys getting together for a bit of fun. Ike would have a strip of celluloid, Spike a camera his uncle had given him for Christmas, Mike would know a friend or two who liked dressing-up and having their photographs taken, and with these modest assets they would club together their pocket money and start the Finer and Supremer Films Corporation. And as for bothering about getting anyone to write them a story, it never occurred to them. They made it up themselves as they went along.

The talkies changed all that. It was no longer possible just to put on a toga, have someone press a button and call the result *The Grandeur that was Rome* or *In the Days of Nero*. A whole elaborate new organization was required. You had to have a studio Boss to boss the Producer, a Producer to produce the Supervisor, a Supervisor to supervise the sub-Supervisor, a sub-Supervisor to sub-supervise the Director, a Director to direct the Cameraman and an Assistant Director to assist the Director. And, above all, you had to get hold of someone to supply the words.

The result was a terrible shortage of authors in all the world's literary centres. New York till then had been full of them. You would see them frisking in perfect masses in any editorial office you happened to enter. Their sharp, excited yapping was one of the features of the first- or second-act interval of every new play that was produced. And in places like Greenwich Village you had to watch your step very carefully to avoid treading on them.

And then all of a sudden all you saw was an occasional isolated one being shooed out of a publisher's sanctum or sitting in a speak-easy sniffing at his press clippings. Time after time fanciers would come up to you with hard-luck stories.

'You know that novelist of mine with the flapping ears and the spots on his coat? Well, he's gone.'

'Gone?'

'Absolutely vanished. I left him on the steps of the club, and when I came out there were no signs of him.'

'Same here,' says another fancier. 'I had a brace of playwrights to whom I was greatly attached, and they've disappeared without a word.'

Well, of course, people took it for granted that the little fellows had strayed and had got run over, for authors are notoriously dreamy in traffic and, however carefully you train them, will persist in stopping in the middle of the street to jot down strong bits of dialogue. It was only gradually that the truth came out. They had all been decoyed away to Hollywood.

What generally happened was this. A couple of the big film executives – say Mr Louis B. Mayer and Mr Adolf Zukor – would sight their quarry in the street and track him down to some bohemian eating resort. Having watched him settle, they seat themselves at a table immediately behind him, and for a few moments there is silence, broken only by the sound of the author eating corned beef hash. Then Mr Mayer addresses Mr Zukor, raising his voice slightly.

'Whatever was the name of that girl?' he says.

'What girl?' asks Mr Zukor, cleverly taking his cue.

'That tall, blonde girl with the large blue eyes.'

'The one in the pink bathing suit?'

'That's right. With the freckle in the small of her back.'

'A freckle? A mole, I always understood.'

'No, it was a freckle, eye-witnesses tell me. Just over the base of the spinal cord. Well, anyway, what was her name?'

'Now what was it? Eulalie something? Clarice something?

No, it's gone. But I'll find out for you when we get home. I know her intimately.'

Here they pause, but not for long. There is a sound of quick, emotional breathing. The author is standing beside them, a rapt expression on his face.

'Pardon me, gentlemen,' he says, 'for interrupting a private conversation, but I chanced to overhear you saying that you were intimately acquainted with a tall, blonde girl with large blue eyes, in the habit of wearing bathing suits of just the type I like best. It is for a girl of that description that I have been scouring the country for years. Where may she be found?'

'In God's Back Garden – Hollywood,' says Mr Zukor.

'Pity you can't meet her,' says Mr Mayer. 'You're just her type.'

'If you were by any chance an author,' says Mr Zukor, 'we could take you back with us tomorrow. Too bad you're not.'

'Prepare yourself for a surprise, gentlemen,' says the victim. 'I *am* an author. George Montague Breamworthy. "Powerfully devised situations" – *New York Times*. "Sheer, stark realism" – *New York Herald-Tribune*. "Whoops!" – *Women's Wear*.'

'In that case,' says Mr Mayer, producing a contract, 'sign here.'

'Where my thumb is,' says Mr Zukor.

The trap has snapped.


## II

That was how they got me, and it was, I understand, the usual method of approach. But sometimes this plan failed, and then sterner methods were employed. The demand for authors in those early talkie days was so great that it led to the revival of the old press-gang. Nobody was safe even if he merely looked like an author.

While having a Malted Milk Greta Garbo with some of the old lags in the commissary one morning about half-way through my term of sentence, I was told of one very interesting case. It appeared that there was a man who had gone out West hoping to locate oil. One of those men without a thought in the world outside of oil, the last thing he had ever dreamed of doing was being an author. With the exception of letters and an occasional telegram of greeting to some relative at Christmas, he had never written anything in his life.

But by some curious chance it happened that his appearance was that of one capable of the highest feats in the way of literary expression. He had a domelike head, piercing eyes, and that cynical twist of the upper lip which generally means an epigram on the way. Still, as I say, he was not a writer, and no one could have been more surprised than he when, walking along a deserted street in Los Angeles, thinking of oil, he was suddenly set upon by masked men, chloroformed, and whisked away in a closed car. When he came to himself he was in a cell on the Perfector-Zizzbaum lot with paper and a sharpened pencil before him, and stern-featured men in felt hats and raincoats were waggling rubber hoses at him and telling him to get busy and turn out something with lots of sex in it, but not too much, because of Will Hays.

The story has a curious sequel. A philosopher at heart, he accepted the situation. He wrenched his mind away from oil and scribbled a few sentences that happened to occur to him. He found, as so many have found, that an author's is the easiest job in existence, and soon he was scratching away as briskly as you could wish. And that is how Noël Coward got his start.

But not every kidnapped author accepted his fate so equably. The majority endeavoured to escape. But it was useless. Even if the rigours of the pitiless California climate did not drive them back to shelter, capture was inevitable. When I was in Hollywood there was much indignation among the better element of the community over the pursuit of an unfortunate woman writer whom the harshness of her supervisor, a man of the name of Legree, had driven to desperation. As I got the story, they chased her across the ice with bloodhounds.

The whole affair was very unpleasant and shocked the soft-hearted greatly. So much so that a Mrs Harriet Beecher Stowe told me that if MGM would meet her terms for the movie, she intended to write a book about it which would stir the world.

'Boy,' she said to me, 'it will be a scorcher!'

I don't know if anything ever came of it.

## III

I got away from Hollywood at the end of the year because the gaoler's daughter smuggled me in a file in a meat pie, but I was there long enough to realize what a terribly demoralizing place it is. The whole atmosphere there is one of insidious deceit and subterfuge. Nothing is what it affects to be. What looks like a tree is really a slab of wood backed with barrels. What appears on the screen as the towering palace of Haroun al-Raschid is actually a cardboard model occupying four feet by three of space. The languorous lagoon is simply a smelly tank with a stagehand named Ed wading about it in bathing trunks.

It is surely not difficult to imagine the effect of all this on a sensitive-minded author. Taught at his mother's knee to love the truth, he finds himself surrounded by people making fortunes by what can only be called chicanery. After a month or two in such an environment could you trust that author to count his golf shots correctly or to give his right sales figures?

And then there was – I am speaking of the old days. It is possible that modern enlightened thought has brought improvements – the inevitable sapping of his self-respect. At the time of which I am writing authors in Hollywood were kept in little hutches. In every studio there were rows and rows of these, each containing an author on a long contract at a weekly salary. You could see their anxious little faces peering out through the bars and hear them whining piteously to be taken for a walk. One had to be very callous not to be touched by such a spectacle.

I do not say that these authors were actually badly treated. In the best studios in those early talkie days kindness was the rule. Often you would see some high executive stop and give one of them a lettuce. And it was the same with the humaner type of director. In fact, between the directors and their authors there frequently existed a rather touching friendship. I remember one director telling a story which illustrates this.

One morning, he said, he was on his way to his office, pre-occupied, as was his habit when planning out the day's work, when he felt a sudden tug at his coat-tails. He looked down and there was his pet author, Edgar Montrose (Book Society – Recommendation) Delamere. The little fellow had got him in a firm grip and was gazing up at him, in his eyes an almost human expression of warning.

Well, the director, not unnaturally, mistook this at first for mere playfulness, for it was often his kindly habit to romp with his little charges. Then something seemed to whisper to him that he was being withheld from some great peril. He remembered stories he had read as a boy – one of which he was even then directing for Rin-Tin-Tin – where faithful dogs dragged their masters back from the brink of precipices on dark nights, and, scarcely knowing why, he turned and went off to the commissary, and had a Strawberry and Vanilla Nut Sundae Mary Pickford.

It was well that he did. In his office, waiting to spring, there was lurking a foreign star with a bad case of temperament, whose bite might have been fatal. You may be sure that Edgar Montrose had a good meal that night.

But that was an isolated case. Not all directors were like this one. Too many of them crushed the spirit of the captives by incessant blue-pencilling of their dialogue, causing them to become listless and lose appetite. Destructive criticism is what kills an author. Cut his material too much, make him feel that he is not a Voice, give him the impression that his big scene is all wet, and you will soon see the sparkle die out of his eyes.

I don't know how conditions are today, but at that time there were authors who had been on salary for years in Hollywood without ever having a line of their work used. All they did was attend story conferences. There were other authors whom nobody had seen for years. It was like the Bastille. They just sat in some hutch away in a corner somewhere and grew white beards and languished. From time to time somebody would renew their contract, and then they were forgotten again.

As I say, it may be different now. After all, I am speaking of twenty-five years ago. But I do think it would be wise if author-fanciers exercised vigilance. You never know. The press-gang may still be in our midst.

So when you take your pet for a walk, keep an eye on him. If he goes sniffing after strange men, whistle him back.

And remember that the spring is the dangerous time. Around

about the beginning of May, authors get restless and start dreaming about girls in abbreviated bathing suits. It is easy to detect the symptoms. The moment you hear yours muttering about the Golden West and God's Sunshine and Out There Beyond The Stifling City put sulphur in his absinthe and lock him up in the kitchenette.

I

And now, Ho for a chapter on the theatre and what I have done to put it on the map.

A dramatist friend of mine was telling me the other day that he had written his last play. He was embittered because the star for whom he had been waiting for two years backed out on obtaining a big television contract and another star for whom he had been waiting two years before that suddenly went off to Hollywood. And this after he had worked like a beaver rewriting his play to suit the views of the manager, the manager's wife, the principal backer and the principal backer's son, a boy of some fourteen summers named Harold, on whose judgement the principal backer placed great reliance.

Furthermore, he said, he could no longer face those out-of-town preliminary tours, with their 'Nobody comes to the theatre on Monday in these small towns. Wait till Tuesday.' 'Well, Tuesday, everyone knows, is a bad night everywhere. Wait till Wednesday,' and 'You can't get 'em into the theatre on a Wednesday. Wait till Thursday. Thursday will tell the story.' And always the manager at his elbow, chewing two inches of an unlighted cigar and muttering, 'Well, boy, there ain't no doubt but what it's going to need a lot of work.'

Myself, I have never regretted my flirtations with the drama.

They cost me a lot of mental anguish, not to mention making me lose so much hair that nowadays I am often mistaken in a dim light for Yul Brynner, but one met such interesting people. I have encountered in the coulisses enough Unforgettable Characters to fix up the *Reader's Digest* for years and years. Most of these are enshrined in the pages of *Bring on the Girls*.

My first play was written in collaboration with a boy named Henry Cullimore when I was seven. I don't quite know what made us decide to do it, but we did so decide, and Henry said we would have to have a plot. 'What's a plot?' I asked. He didn't know. He had read or heard somewhere that a plot was a good thing to have, but as to what it was he confessed himself fogged. This naturally made us both feel a little dubious as to the outcome of our enterprise, but we agreed that there was nothing to do but carry on and hope that everything would pan out all right. (Chekhov used to do this.)

He – Henry Cullimore, not Chekhov – was the senior partner in the project. He was two or three years older than I was, which gave him an edge, and he had a fountain-pen. I mostly contributed moral support, pursuing the same method which I later found to answer so well when I teamed up with Guy Bolton. When Guy and I pitched in on a play, he would do the rough spadework – the writing – and I used to look in on him from time to time and say 'How are you getting on?' He would say, 'All right,' and I would say, 'Fine,' and go off and read Agatha Christie. Giving it the Wodehouse Touch, I used to call it. And so little by little and bit by bit the thing would get done.

This system worked capitally with all the Bolton–Wodehouse productions, and I believe it was the way Beaumont and Fletcher used to hammer out their combined efforts. ('How goeth it, my heart of gold?' 'Yarely, old mole. Well, fairly yarely.' 'Stick at it, boy. Hard work never hurt anyone.') But Henry Cullimore let me down. A broken reed, if ever there was one. He got as far as

## ACT ONE

*[Enter Henry]*

HENRY: What's for breakfast? Ham and oatmeal?

Very nice.

but there he stopped. He had shot his bolt.

How he was planning to go on if inspiration had not blown a fuse, I never discovered. I should imagine that the oatmeal would have proved to be poisoned – ('One of the barbiturate group, Inspector, unless I am greatly mistaken') – or a dead body would have dropped out of the closet where they kept the sugar.

The thing was never produced. A pity, for I think it would have been a great audience show.

Since then I have been mixed up in sixteen straight plays and twenty-two musical comedies as author, part author or just hanging on to the author in the capacity of Charles his friend. In virtually every theatrical enterprise there is a Charles his friend, drawing his weekly royalties. Nobody ever quite knows how he wriggled in, but there he is. Affability of manner has a good deal to do with it.

But though I attached myself to these straight plays, some of them the most outstanding flops in the history of the stage, my heart was never really in them. Musical comedy was my dish, the musical-comedy theatre my spiritual home. I would rather have written *Oklahoma!* than *Hamlet*. (Actually, as the records show, I wrote neither, but you get the idea.)

It was in 1904 that I burst on the theatrical scene with a lyric in a thing called *Sergeant Brue* at the Prince of Wales Theatre in London. In 1906 I got a job at £2 a week as a sort of utility lyricist at the Aldwych Theatre in the same town. This, as I have already recorded, involved writing some numbers with a young American composer named Jerome Kern, and when, a good many years later, I ran into him and Guy Bolton in New York, we got together and did those Princess Theatre shows. After that I worked with Victor Herbert, George Gershwin, Rudolf Friml, Sigmund Romberg, Vincent Youmans, Emmerich Kalman, Ivan Caryll, Franz Lehár and what seems to me now about a hundred other composers. For years scarcely a day passed whose low descending sun did not see me at my desk trying to find some rhyme for 'June' that would not be 'soon', 'moon', 'tune' or 'spoon'. (One bright young man suddenly thought of 'macaroon' and soared right away to the top of the profession.)

It is not to be wondered at, then, that when I can spare a moment of my valuable time, I find myself brooding on the New York musical-comedy theatre of today. The subject is one of compelling interest. What is going to happen to it? Can it last? If so, how much longer? Will there come a day when we reach out for it and find it isn't there? Are the rising costs of production ever going to stop rising? It is difficult enough to prise the required $250,000 out of the investing public now. What of tomorrow, when it will probably be half a million?

Have you ever tried to touch anyone for $250,000? It is by no means the same thing as asking for a fiver till Wednesday, old man. It takes doing. Howard Dietz, the lyrist, once wrote an opening chorus for a revue which was produced by a prominent Broadway producer called Max Gordon. It ran:

> What's all that cheering in the streets?
> What's all that cheering you're hearing in the streets?
> Max Gordon's raised the money,
> Max Gordon's raised the money...

and while joining in the cheering, one cannot help dropping a silent tear as one thinks of what Max must have gone through. And in his capacity of prominent Broadway manager, he presumably had to do it again and again and again.

How anyone who had once raised the money for a New York musical can bring himself to do it a second time is more than I can imagine. A few years ago a management decided that the moment had come to revive a show with which I had been connected somewhere around 1920 and asked me to look in at 'backers' audition'. I was there through the grim proceedings, and came away feeling like one of those can-you-spare-a-nickel-for-a-cup-of-coffee gentlemen of leisure who pop up through the sidewalk in front of you as you take your walks abroad in New York's seedier districts. My hat, quite a good one, seemed battered and shapeless, there were cracks in the uppers of my shoes, and an unwholesome growth of hair had sprouted on my cheeks, accompanied by a redness and swelling of the nose. I felt soiled. (There were headlines in all the papers – WODEHOUSE FEELS SOILED.)

A backers' audition is composed of cringing mendicants – the management, a pianist, some hired singers and some friends and supporters who are there to laugh and applaud – and a little group of fat, rich men with tight lips and faces carved out of granite, whom you have assembled somehow and herded into a hotel suite. These are the backers, or it might be better to say you hope they are the backers, for while there is unquestionably gold in them thar heels, the problem is how to extract it.

Cigars, drinks and caviare have been provided, and the management proceeds to read the script, pausing at intervals to allow the hired singers to render the songs. The fat, rich men sit there with their eyes bulging, in a silence broken only by the champing of jaws and a musical gurgle as another whisky and soda goes down the gullet, and then, loaded to the Plimsoll mark with caviare, they file out, not having uttered a word.

And this goes on and on. In order to collect the money to produce *Oklahoma!* eighty-nine of these auditions had to be given. I imagine that it was not till about the sixty-third that somebody stirred in his chair and brought out a cheque-book. Perhaps one of the songs had touched his heart, reminding him of something his mother used to sing when he clustered about her knee, or possibly conscience whispered to him that as he was all that caviare ahead of the game, he ought to do something about it. So he wrote his cheque.

But for how much? $10,000? $20,000? Even if it was $50,000, it would only have scratched the surface. *Oklahoma!* was $20,000 short when it opened out of town, and would never have been brought into New York if S. N. Behrman, the playwright, had not come to the rescue.

However, let us suppose that somehow you have contrived to wheedle $250,000 out of the moneyed classes. What then? You are then faced with the prospect of having to play to $33,000 a week simply to break even. I was shown the weekly balance sheet of an apparently very prosperous Broadway musical comedy the other day. The gross box-office receipts were $36,442.90, which sounds fine, but after all expenses had been paid the profit on the week was $3697.83. I am no mathematician, but it looked to me as if they would have to go on doing about $37,000 a week for about a year and a half before the backers drew a cent. No wonder these prudent men are often inclined to settle for free cigars and caviare and not get mixed up in all that sordid business of paying out money.

That is why if you ever catch me in pensive mood, sitting

with chin supported in the hand and the elbow on the knee, like Rodin's 'Thinker', you can be pretty sure that I am saying to myself, 'Whither the New York musical-comedy theatre?' or, possibly, 'The New York musical-comedy theatre ... whither?' It is a question that constantly exercises me. I can't see what, as the years roll by and costs continue to rise, is going to happen to the bally thing.

## II

It is the stagehand situation that causes a good deal of the present unrest. This situation – I am speaking of the stagehand situation – is quite a situation. The trouble, briefly, is this. Stagehands cost money, and theatrical managers hate parting with money. The scene-shifters' union, on the other hand, is all for it. Blow the expense, says the scene-shifters' union. It likes to see money in handfuls scattered, always provided it is someone else's (or someone's else, as the case may be). This leads to strained relations, pique on both sides and the calling of some most unpleasant names. I have heard managers refer to the union as vampires, while the union, speaking of the managers, is far too prone to make nasty cracks about people who are so tight they could carry an armful of eels up six flights of stairs and never drop one of them.

Most plays nowadays are in one set, and a manager who puts on a one-set play feels that once this one set is in position he ought to be able to pay the scene-shifters off and kiss them good-bye. He sees no reason why he should have to pay a weekly wage to a gang of scene-shifters just for not shifting scenes. All he wants is an operative who will go over the set from time to time with a feather duster, to keep the moths from getting into it.

The union does not take this view. It holds that if the manager hasn't any scenes to shift he jolly well ought to have, and it insists on him employing the number of scene-shifters who would have been required to shift the scenes if there had been any scenes to shift, if you follow me. And as any attempt to brook the will of the union leads to a strike of stagehands, which leads to a strike of electricians, which leads to a strike of actors, box-office officials, gentlemanly ushers and the theatre cat, it gets its way. Thus we find Victor Borge, giving a two-hour solo performance on the piano at the Booth, obliged to supply eight stagehands. And a recent one-set comedy with three characters in it was attended nightly by no fewer than fifteen admirers and well-wishers. Some plays these last seasons have suffered from audience thinness, but no manager has ever run short of stagehands. They are there from the moment the curtain goes up, with their hair in a braid.

At a risk of becoming too technical, I must explain briefly how a troupe of stagehands with nothing to do is organized. There is, I need scarcely say, nothing haphazard about it. First – chosen by show of hands (stagehands) – comes the head man or Giant Sloth. His job is to hang upside down from a rafter. Next we have the Senior Lounger and the Junior Lounger, who lie on couches – Roman fashion – with chaplets of roses round their foreheads. Last come the rank and file, the twelve Lilies of the Field. It was because I was uncertain as to the duties of these that I looked in the other night at one of the theatres to get myself straight on the point, and was courteously received by the Junior Lounger, a Mr B. J. Wilberforce, who showed no annoyance at being interrupted while working on his crossword puzzle.

'I was wondering, Mr Wilberforce,' I said, when greetings and compliments had been exchanged, 'if you could tell me something about this situation?'

'What situation would that be?' he asked.

'The scene-shifter situation,' I said, and he frowned.

'We prefer not to be called scene-shifters,' he explained. 'There seems to us something a little vulgar about shifting scenes. It smacks too much of those elaborate musical productions, where, I am told, the boys often get quite hot and dusty. We of the elite like to think of ourselves as America's leisure class. Of course, when there is work to be done, we do it. Only the other night, for instance, the producer thought that it would brighten things up if an upstage chair were moved to a downstage position. We were called into conference, and long before the curtain rose for the evening's performance the thing was done. Superintended by the Giant Sloth, we Loungers – myself and my immediate superior, Cyril Muspratt – each grasped one side of the seat and that chair was moved, and it would have been the same if it had been two chairs. I am not saying it did not take it out of us. It did. But we do not spare ourselves when the call comes.'

'Still, it does not come often, I suppose? As a general rule, you have your leisure?'

'Oh, yes. We have lots of time to fool around in.'

'Never end a sentence with a preposition, Wilberforce,' I said warningly, and he blushed. I had spoken kindly, but you could see it stung.

At this moment somebody on the stage said in a loud voice, 'My God! My Wife!' – they were playing one of those Victorian farce revivals designed to catch the nostalgia trade – and he winced.

'All this noise!' he sad. 'One realizes that actors have to make a living, but there is no need for a lot of racket and disturbance. It is most disagreeable for a man doing his crossword puzzle and trying to concentrate on a word in three letters beginning with E and signifying "large Australian bird" to be distracted by sudden sharp cries. Still, it might be worse. At the Bijou, where they are doing one of those gangster things, the Giant Sloth was often woken three or four times in an evening by pistol-shots. He had to complain about it, and now, I believe, the actors just say, "Bang, Bang!" in an undertone. Three letters beginning with E,' he mused.

I knew it could not be the Sun God Ra. Then suddenly I got it. 'Emu!'

'I beg your pardon?'

'That large Australian bird you were speaking of.'

'Of which you were speaking. Never end a sentence with a preposition, Wodehouse.'

It was my turn to blush, and my face was still suffused when we were joined by an impressive-looking man in slacks and a sleeveless vest. This proved to be Cyril Muspratt, the Senior Lounger.

'And do you, too, do crossword puzzles, Mr Muspratt?' I asked when introductions had been concluded.

He shook his head laughingly, looking bronzed and fit.

'I am more the dreamer type,' he said. 'I like to sit and think . . . well, anyway, sit. I read a good deal, too. What do you think of this bird Kafka?'

'What do you?'

'I asked you first,' he said with a touch of warmth, and sensing that tempers were rising I bade them good night and went on my way. So I still don't know how those Lilies of the Field fill in their time. Hide-and-seek, perhaps? The dark back of the theatre would be splendid for hide-and-seek. Or leap-frog? Perhaps they just catch up with their reading, like Mr Muspratt.

They tell a tale in Shubert Alley of a manager who walked one day on Forty-Fifth Street west of Broadway and paused to watch workmen razing the Avon Theatre.

'Gosh!' he said, much moved. 'They're using fewer men to tear down the building than we used to have to hire to strike a one-set show.'

And there, gentle reader, let us leave him.

## III

But to a certain extent, I think, the troubles of the New York theatre must be attributed to the peculiar methods of the box-office officials. They seem to go out of their way to make it difficult for the public to buy seats. A lady living in Farmingdale, New Jersey, recently wrote to the box-office of one of the play-houses as follows:

Please send me four tickets at $4 for any Saturday evening. Cheque for $16 enclosed.

To which she received the reply:

There are no $2 seats on Saturday evenings.

She then wrote:

Please re-read my letter and cheque.

The theatre riposted:

There are no $2 seats on Saturday evenings.

Passions run hot in Farmingdale, NJ. The lady came back with a stinker:

I cannot understand what the difficulty is. Who on earth said anything about $2 seats? I wrote asking you for four seats at $4 each. I enclosed a cheque for $16. Four times four are sixteen. Nobody wants $2 seats, asked for them or sent a cheque for them. Please send me the tickets.

Did this rattle the box-office man? Did he blush and shuffle his feet? No, sir. His letter in reply read as follows:

There are no $2 seats on Saturday evenings.

I

Looking back over what I have written, J.P., I see that I have not really covered that question you asked about the changes I notice now in the American scene. I spoke, you may remember, of the wonderful improvement there has been of late in American manners but I omitted to touch on those equally intriguing subjects, the recent upheaval in the world of divorce and the present swollen condition of the American Christmas. Both deserve more than a passing word.

The American Christmas is very different today from what it was when, a piefaced lad in my twenties, I first trod the sidewalks of New York. Then a simple festival, it now seems to have got elephantiasis or something. I don't want to do anyone an injustice, but the thought has sometimes crossed my mind that some of the big department stores are trying to make money out of Christmas. I cannot help thinking that to certain persons in New York – I name no names – Christmas is not just a season of homely goodwill but an opportunity to gouge the populace out of what little savings it has managed to accumulate in the past year. All those Santa Clauses you see. I feel they are there for a purpose.

Christmas in New York brings out the Santa Clauses like flies.

Go into any big department store, and there is a Santa Claus sitting in a chair with children crawling all over him. 'Our humble heroes!' are the words that spring to my lips as I see them, for these stores are always superheated, and you cannot be a Santa Claus without padding yourself liberally about the middle. At the end of the day these devoted men must feel like Shadrach, Meshach and Abednego, and also probably not unlike King Herod, of whose forthright methods I have heard several of them speak with wistful admiration.

I interviewed one of them the other day in a restaurant whither he had gone in his brief time off to refresh himself with a quick wassail bowl.

'Don't you ever falter?' I asked.

He gave me a look.

'A Santa Claus who faltered,' he replied stiffly, 'would receive short shrift from his co-workers. Next morning at daybreak he would find himself in a hollow square of his fellow-Clauses, being formally stripped of his beard and stomach padding. We are a proud guild, we Santas, and we brook no weakness. Besides,' he went on, 'though the life of a department-store Santa Claus is admittedly fraught with peril, he can console himself with the reflection that he is by no means as badly off as the shock troops of the profession, the men who have to go into the offices. Take the case of a department-store Santa Claus in whose whiskers a child has deposited his semi-liquefied chewing-gum. A man who has had to comb chewing-gum – or for the matter of that milk chocolate – out of the undergrowth at the close of his working day becomes a graver, deeper man. He has seen life. And he knows he has got to go through it again tomorrow. But does he quail?'

'Doesn't he quail?'

'No, sir, he does not quail. He says to himself that what he is suffering is as nothing compared to what a man like, for instance, Butch Oberholtzer has to face. Butch is the Santa attached to a prominent monthly magazine, and it is his task to circulate among the advertisers during Christmas week and give them a hearty seasonal greeting from his employers. Well, you know what sort of condition the average advertiser is in during Christmas week, after those daily office parties. Let so much as a small fly stamp its feet suddenly on the ceiling and he leaps like a stricken blancmange. You can picture his emotions, then, when as he sits quivering in his chair a Santa Claus steals up behind him, slaps him on the back and shouts, "Merry Christmas, old boy, merry Christmas!" On several occasions Butch has escaped with his life by the merest hair's-breadth. I wonder if his luck can last?'

'Let us hope so,' I said soberly.

He shrugged his shoulders.

'Ah well,' he said, 'if the worst happens, it will be just one more grave among the hills.'

This man told me one thing that shocked me a good deal. For years I have been worrying myself sick, wondering why yaks' tails were imported into the United States from Tibet. I could not understand there being any popular demand for them. I know that if someone came up to me and said, 'Mr Wodehouse, I have long been a great admirer of your work and would like to do something by way of a small return for all the happy hours you have given me. Take this yak's tail, and make it a constant companion,' I would thank him and giggle a little and say how frightfully good of him and it was just what I had been wanting, but I should most certainly try to lose the thing on my way home. And I would have supposed that a similar distaste for these objects prevailed almost universally.

I now have the facts. Yaks' tails are used for making beards for department-store Santa Clauses, and I can never again feel quite the same about the department-store Santa Claus. His white beard, once venerable, now revolts me. Looking at it, I find a picture rising before my eyes of some unfortunate yak wandering about Tibet without a tail. You don't have to know much about the sensitive nature of the yak to realize what this must mean to the bereaved animal. It is bathed in confusion. It doesn't know which way to look.

But let us leave a distasteful subject and get on to the recent alarming slump in America's divorce rate.

## II

In the realm of sport America has not been doing too well of late. The Davis Cup has gone to Australia again, and now the World Bridge Championship, played at the Hotel Claridge, Paris, is over, and the French team, headed by the Messieurs Pierre Ghestem and René Bacherich, are whooping and throwing their berets in the air, while Charles Goren, Lee Hazen and the other representatives of the United States sit huddled in a corner, telling one another that, after all, it is only a game.

The result apparently was against all the ruling of the form book, and I wish I knew more about Bridge, so that I could give you an expert analysis of the run of the play. All I have to go on is what Mr Hazen told an interviewer at the close of the proceedings.

'We in America,' said Mr Hazen, 'are used to playing with a conventional system. But the French have borrowed from the Viennese, the Swedish and the Norwegian.'

Well, naturally, an American who sits down to play Bridge with a Frenchman expects him to play *like* a Frenchman. It disconcerts him when the other suddenly tears off his whiskers and shouts, 'April fool! I'm a Norwegian!' He is bewildered and at a loss. He forgets what are trumps and even, if of a particularly nervous temperament, forgets that he is playing Bridge at all and keeps saying 'Snap!' every time a card is laid down. You can't win world tournaments that way.

Still more unsettling to the American team must have been the conditions under which the matches were played.

'The French system,' said Mr Hazen, 'is based on no interference.'

One sees what this means. When you play Bridge in France you do it in an atmosphere of cloistral calm, broken only by an occasional murmured 'Nice work, old man' (*Joli travail, mon vieux*), 'At-a-boy!' (*Voilà le garçon*) and so on, and it would obviously take Americans, accustomed to the more boisterous ways of their native land, a long time to get used to this. Back home there was all the hurly-burly associated with the baseball arena, and without an audience shouting 'Take him out!' 'Who ever told you you could play Bridge, ya big stiff?' and the like, the American team was ill at ease and off its game.

Well, as they keep saying, it is only a pastime and these things cannot affect us finally, but any observer who is at all keen-eyed can see that Charles Goren and Lee Hazen are good and sore, as are their colleagues, and there has been some rather sharp criticism of Jeff Glick, the non-playing captain of the American team, for not having seen to it that the playing members had a few of those extra aces up their sleeves which make so much difference in a closely contested chukker.

However, Davis Cups and Bridge championships are not

everything, and the downhearted were able to console themselves with the reflection that, whatever might happen on the tennis court or at the card-table, in one field of sport America still led the world. Her supremacy in the matter of Divorce remained unchallenged. Patriots pointed with pride at the figures, which showed that while thirteen in every thousand American ever-loving couples decided each year to give their chosen mates the old heave-ho, the best, the nearest competitor, Switzerland, could do was three.

'As long as we have Texas oil millionaires, Hollywood film stars and Tommy Manville,' people told one another, 'we're all right. Come the three corners of the world in arms, and we shall shock them.'

And, of course, at times they did, considerably.

But now the whole situation has changed. We learn from the New York *Daily Mirror* that, 'An amazing thing has been happening, little noticed, in our national life. Since 1946 there has been a forty per cent decline in the number of divorces.' Just like that. No preparation, no leading up to it, no attempt to break the thing gently. It is as if the *Mirror* had crept up behind America and struck her on the back of the head with a sock full of wet sand.

The paper omits to mention what is happening in Switzerland, but one assumes that the Swiss are still plugging along in the old dogged way and by this time may have got up to five per thousand or even six. For don't run away with the idea that the Swiss do nothing but yodel and make condensed milk. They have plenty of leisure, be well assured, for divorce actions. Probably at this very moment some citizen of the inland republic is in the witness-box showing the judge the bump on his head where the little woman hit him with the cuckoo clock. And

America still sunk in complacency and over-confidence. It is the old story of the tortoise and the hare.

Well, the facts are out, but it is difficult to know where to place the blame. Certainly not on Hollywood. The spirit of the men (and the women) there is splendid. Every day one reads in the gossip columns another of those heart-warming announcements to the effect that Lotta Svelte and George Marsupial are holding hands and plan to merge as soon as the former can disentangle herself from Marcus Manleigh and the latter from Belinda Button, and one knows that George and Lotta are not going to let the side down. In due season she will be in court telling the judge that for a fortnight the marriage was a very happy one, but then George started reading the paper at breakfast and refusing to listen when she told him of the dream she had had last night, thus causing her deep mental agony. No, the heart of Hollywood is sound. So is that of the Texas oil men. And nobody can say that Tommy Manville is not trying.

It may be that it is the judges who are lacking in team spirit. A great deal must always depend on the judges. Some of them are all right. Not a word of complaint about the one in Hackensack, New Jersey, who recently granted Mrs Carmella Porretta a divorce because her husband, Salvatore, struck her with a buttered muffin. But what are we to say of the judge who, when Mrs Edna Hunt Tankersley applied to him for her twelfth divorce, callously informed her that as far as he was concerned she got her 'final final decree'? In other words, when this splendid woman, all eagerness to see America first, comes up for the thirteenth time, her industry and determination will be unrewarded. No Baker's dozen for Edna, unless, of course, she is shrewd enough to take her custom elsewhere.

Has this judge never reflected that it is just this sort of thing that discourages ambition and is going to hand the world's leadership to the Swiss on a plate with watercress round it? Can one be surprised that the Swiss, who pull together as one man in every patriotic movement, are steadily creeping up and likely to forge ahead at any moment?

A theory held by some to account for this distressing decline in the divorce rate in the United States is that the modern American husband, instead of getting a divorce, finds it cheaper to dissect his bride with the meat axe and deposit the debris in a sack in the Jersey marshes. I doubt it. One has heard, of course, of the man in Chicago named Young who once, when his nerves were unstrung, put his wife Josephine in the chopping machine and canned her and labelled her 'Tongue', but as a rule the American wife does not murder easy. A story now going the rounds bears this out, the story of the husband and wife in California.

For three or four days, it seems, the marriage between this young couple had been an ideally happy one, but then, as so often happens, the husband became restless and anxious for a change. At first he thought of divorce, and then he thought again and remembered that in California there is a community law which gives the sundered wife half the family property. And he was just reconciling himself to putting a new coat of paint on her and trying to make her do for another year, when an idea struck him.

Why not say it with rattlesnakes?

So he got a rattlesnake and put it in the pocket of his trousers and hung the trousers over a chair in the bedroom, and when his wife asked him for some money, he told her she would find his wallet in his trouser pocket.

'In the bedroom,' he said, and she went into the bedroom, whence her voice presently emerged.

'Which trousers?'

'The grey ones.'

'The ones hanging on the chair?'

'That's right.'

'Which pocket?'

'The hip pocket.'

'But I've looked there,' said his wife discontentedly, 'and all I could find was a rattlesnake.'

## I

And now, to conclude, I see that you ask me to tell you what are my methods of work, and I am wondering if here your questionnaire has not slipped a cog and gone off the right lines. Are you sure your radio and newspaper public want to know?

I ask because I have never been able to make myself believe that anything about my methods of work can possibly be of interest to anyone. Sometimes on television I have been lured into describing them, and always I have had the feeling that somebody was going to interrupt with that line of Jack Benny's – 'There will now be a slight pause while everyone says "Who cares?" ' I should have said that if there was one subject on which the world would prefer not to be informed, it was this.

Still, if you really think the boys and girls are anxious to get the inside facts, let's go.

I would like to say, as I have known other authors to say, that I am at my desk every morning at nine sharp, but something tells me I could never get away with it. The newspaper and radio public is a shrewd public, and it knows that no one is ever at his desk at nine. I do get to my desk, however, round about ten, and everything depends then on whether or not I put my feet up on it. If I do, I instantly fall into a reverie or coma, musing on ships and shoes and sealing wax and cabbages and kings. My mind drifts off into the past and, like the man in the Bab Ballads, I wonder how the playmates of my youth are getting on – McConnell, S. B. Walters, Paddy Byles and Robinson. This goes on for some time. Many of my deepest thoughts have come to me when I have my feet up on the desk, but I have never been able to fit one of them into any novel I have been writing.

If I avoid this snare, I pull chair up to typewriter, adjust the Peke which is lying on my lap, chirrup to the foxhound, throw a passing pleasantry to the cat and pitch in.

All the animal members of the household take a great interest in my literary work, and it is rare for me to begin the proceedings without a quorum. I sometimes think I could concentrate better in solitude, and I wish particularly that the cat would give me a word of warning before jumping on the back of my neck as I sit trying to find the *mot juste*, but I remind myself that conditions might be worse. I might be dictating my stuff.

How anybody can compose a story by word of mouth face to face with a bored-looking secretary with a notebook is more than I can imagine. Yet many authors think nothing of saying, 'Ready, Miss Spelvin? Take dictation. Quote No comma Sir Jasper Murgatroyd comma close quotes comma said no better make it hissed Evangeline comma quote I would not marry you if you were the last man on earth period close quotes Quote Well comma I'm not comma so the point does not arise comma close quotes replied Sir Jasper comma twirling his moustache cynically period. And so the long day wore on period. End of chapter.'

If I had to do that sort of thing I should be feeling all the time that the girl was saying to herself as she took it down, 'Well comma this beats me period. How comma with homes for the feeble-minded touting for custom on every side comma has a man like this succeeded in remaining at large as of even date mark of interrogation.'

Nor would I be more happy and at my ease with one of those machines where you talk into a mouthpiece and have your observations recorded on wax. I bought one of them once and started *Right Ho, Jeeves* on it. I didn't get beyond the first five lines.

*Right Ho, Jeeves*, as you may or may not know, Winkler, begins with the words:

'Jeeves,' I said, 'may I speak frankly?'
'Certainly, sir.'
'What I have to say may wound you.'
'Not at all, sir.'
'Well, then——'

and when I reached the 'Well, then——' I thought I would turn back and play the thing over to hear how it sounded.

There is only one adjective to describe how it sounded, the adjective 'awful'. Until that moment I had never realized that I had a voice like that of a very pompous headmaster addressing the young scholars in his charge from the pulpit in the school chapel, but if this machine was to be relied on, that was the sort of voice I had. There was a kind of foggy dreariness about it that chilled the spirits.

It stunned me. I had been hoping, if all went well, to make *Right Ho, Jeeves* an amusing book – gay, if you see what I mean – rollicking, if you still follow me, and debonair, and it was plain to me that a man with a voice like that could never come within several million light-miles of being gay and debonair. With him at the controls, the thing would develop into one of those dim tragedies of the grey underworld which we return to the library after a quick glance at Chapter One. I sold the machine next day, and felt like the Ancient Mariner when he got rid of the albatross.

## II

My writing, if and when I get down to it, is a combination of longhand and typing. I generally rough out a paragraph or a piece of dialogue in pencil on a pad and then type an improved version. This always answers well unless while using the pad I put my feet up on the desk, for then comes the reverie of which I was speaking and the mind drifts off to other things.

I am fortunate as a writer in not being dependent on my surroundings. Some authors, I understand, can give of their best only if there is a vase of roses of the right shade on the right spot of their desk and away from their desk are unable to function. I have written quite happily on ocean liners during gales, with the typewriter falling into my lap at intervals, in hotel bedrooms, in woodsheds, in punts on lakes, in German internment camps and in the Inspecteurs' room at the Palais de Justice in Paris at the time when the French Republic suspected me of being a danger to it. (Actually, I was very fond of the French Republic and would not have laid a finger on it if you had brought it to me asleep on a chair, but they did not know this.) I suppose it was those seven years when I was doing the 'By The Way' column on the *Globe* that gave me the useful knack of being able to work under any conditions.

Writing my stories – or at any rate rewriting them – I enjoy. It is the thinking them out that puts those dark circles under my eyes. You can't think out plots like mine without getting a suspicion from time to time that something has gone seriously wrong with the brain's two hemispheres and that broad band of transversely running fibres known as the *corpus callosum*. There always comes a moment in the concoction of a scenario when I pause and say to myself, 'Oh, what a noble mind is here o'erthrown.' If somebody like Sir Roderick Glossop could have read the notes I made for my last one – *Something Fishy* – 400 pages of them – he would have been on the telephone instructing two strong men to hurry along with the strait-waistcoat before he was half-way through. I append a few specimens:

*Father an actor? This might lead to something.*
(There is no father in the story.)

*Make brother genial, like Bingo Little's bookie.*
(There is no brother in the story.)

*Crook tells hero and heroine about son.*
(There is no crook in the story, either.)

*Son hairdresser? Skating instructor?*
(There is no son in the story.)

*Can I work it so that somebody – who? – has told her father that she is working as a cook?*

(This must have meant something to me at the time, but the mists have risen and the vision faded.)

*Artist didn't paint picture himself, but knew who painted it. Artist then need not be artist.*

(Who this artist is who has crept into the thing is a mystery to me. He never appears again.)

And finally a note which would certainly have aroused Sir Roderick Glossop's worst suspicions. Coming in the middle of a page with no hint as to why it is there, it runs thus:

*An excellent hair lotion may be made of stewed prunes and isinglass.*

The odd thing is that, just as I am feeling that I must get a proposer and seconder and have myself put up for Colney Hatch, something always clicks and the story straightens itself out, and after that, as in the case of Otis Quackenbush, all is gas and gaiters, not to mention joy and jollity. I shall have to rewrite every line in the book a dozen times, but once I get my scenario set, I know that it is simply a matter of plugging away at it.

To me a detailed scenario is, as they say, of the essence. Some writers will tell you that they just sit down and take pen in hand and let their characters carry on as they see fit. Not for me any procedure like that. I wouldn't trust my characters an inch. If I sat back and let them take charge, heaven knows what the result would be. They have to do just what the scenario tells them to, and no larks. It has always seemed to me that planning a story out and writing it are two separate things. If I were going to run a train, I would feel that the square thing to do was to provide the customers with railway lines and see that the points were in working order. Otherwise – or so I think – I would have my public shouting, as did the lady in Marie Lloyd's immortal song:

> Oh, mister porter,
> What shall I do?
> I want to go to Birmingham
> And they're taking me on to Crewe.

Anyone who reads a novel of mine can be assured that it will be as coherent as I can make it – which, I readily agree, is not saying much, and that, though he may not enjoy the journey, he will get to Birmingham all right.


# III

Well, I think that about cleans the thing up, J.P., does it not? You will have gathered, in case you were worrying, that in my seventy-sixth year – I shall be seventy-six in October – 15th, if you were thinking of sending me some little present – I am still ticking over reasonably briskly. I eat well, sleep well and do not tremble when I see a job of work. In fact, if what you were trying to say in your letter was, 'Hullo there, Wodehouse, how *are* you?' my reply is that I'm fine. Touch of lumbago occasionally in the winter months and a little slow at getting after the dog next door when I see him with his head and shoulders in our garbage can, but otherwise all spooked up with zip and vinegar, as they say out west.

All the same, a letter like yours, with its emphasis on 'over seventy', does rather touch an exposed nerve. It makes one realize that one is not the bright-eyed youngster one had been considering oneself and that shades of the prison house are beginning, as one might put it, to close upon the growing boy. A rude awakening, of course, and one that must have come to my housemaster at school (who recently died at the age of ninety-six) when he said to a new boy on the first day of term: 'Wapshott? Wapshott? That name seems familiar. Wasn't your father in my form?'

'Yes, sir,' replied the stripling. '*And* my grandfather.'

Collapse of old party, as the expression is.

# INDEX